Wordarrows

WORDARROWS

Native States of
Literary Sovereignty

Gerald Vizenor

With a new introduction by the author

UNIVERSITY OF NEBRASKA PRESS
LINCOLN AND LONDON

First Nebraska paperback printing: 2003

Cataloging-in-Publication data available
Library of Congress Control Number: 2002043036
ISBN 0-8032-9629-0 (pbk.: alk. paper)

This Nebraska edition follows the original in
beginning chapter 1 on arabic page 7.

For Robert Vizenor

INTRODUCTION

NATIVE STATES OF LITERARY SOVEREIGNTY

Gerald Vizenor

The native warrior turns an arrow, true and certain, on his teeth with a sense of presence and natural reason, an active, artistic tradition that is heard evermore in stories and is a distinctive mark of literary sovereignty.

Natives are created in words, their sacred names are derived in nature, and their presence is forever related in stories. Natives create the earth, animals, birds, tricksters, shadows, and seasons in their personal visions, memories, names, and stories. Clearly, native traditions arise as a creative practice and are sustained by a crucial sense of presence and survivance in stories.

"The arrowmaker is preeminently the man made of words," said N. Scott Momaday more than thirty years ago at the First Convocation of American Indian Scholars. Momaday, a native artist, author, and teacher, created memorable stories about the significance of language and literature.

"The Kiowas made fine arrows and straightened them in their teeth," said Momaday. "If the arrow is well made, it will have tooth marks upon it."

"Once there was a man and his wife. They were alone at night in their tipi. By the light of the fire the man was making arrows," he told the audience of native scholars.

> There was a small opening in the tipi where two hides had been sewn together. Someone was there on the outside looking in. . . . He took up the arrow and straightened it in his teeth; then as it was right for him to do, he drew it to the bow and took aim. . . . all the while he was talking, as if to his wife.

But this is how he spoke: "I know that you are there on the outside. If you are Kiowa, you will understand what I am saying, and you will speak your name."

But there was no answer, and the man went on in the same way, pointing the arrow all around. At last his aim fell upon the place where his enemy stood, and he let go of the string. The arrow went straight to the enemy's heart.

Momaday related that the arrowmaker existed in words, in the oral tradition, and in a native sense of presence because "language is the repository of his whole knowledge and experience. He was consummate being in language; it is the world of his origin and of his posterity, and there is no other. For the arrowmaker, language represented the only chance for survival."

Native stories are at once survivance.

Momaday concluded that it "is worth considering that he survives in our time, and that he has survived over a period of untold generations." The story of the arrowmaker continues in native memory as a mark of survivance and literary sovereignty.

The first edition of this book was published with the subtitle "Indians and Whites in the New Fur Trade." The metaphor of a "new" fur trade, of course, teased the ironies of natives and others in the historical fur trade of the eighteenth century. The secondary title was an allusion to the dominance of current factors, those recovered, subversive agents who misrepresented natives as outsiders. They were the enemies of the arrowmaker and native survivance.

The original subtitle, however, distracted some readers who thought my stories were related to an actual history of the fur trade. The irony endures by turns, and in this edition the stories are better served with a subtitle that observes the creative states of native storiers, survivance, and literary sovereignty.

I was named the first native executive director of the American Indian Employment and Guidance Center, which was associated with the Waite Neighborhood House in Minneapolis, Minnesota. Natives nominated me over a dominant but sympathetic blond woman who had been offered the position. "We want our own director, one of us, and more tribal people serving on the board," demanded the native activist George Mitchell.

"We have taken chances with Indians and they've let us down," said

Roy Bjorkman, then the chairman of the board and an actual new fur trader. He owned an exclusive fur store in downtown Minneapolis. "Now we must have a white person with executive skills."

"Whose executive skills?" asked Mitchell. "We've been taking chances on you white people for two hundred years or more. We have a right to what you white people do in our name."

I was hired with no executive manners but with extensive experience in the critical resistance to racial simulations and cultural dominance. My initial objectives were to remove the condescending word "guidance" from the name of the organization and to oust the actual and virtual new fur traders who presided on the board of directors. Naturally, my executive moves created resentment and an instant political fury.

Natives ridiculed the invitation to guidance, and most of the new fur traders were eliminated a few months later by shrewd parliamentary maneuvers and amendments to the bylaws of the American Indian Employment Center.

Bower Hawthorne, then executive editor of the *Minneapolis Tribune*, court judges, attorneys, one furrier, and other agents of cultural dominance missed two special sessions of the board. The new bylaws provided the just cause to remove them from the board of directors.

Douglas Hall, a labor union attorney, was elected to the new board of directors because he advocated radical involvement in local politics and supported our protests for native rights. I first misheard his name as Gus Hall, the general secretary of the Communist Party in America. Douglas was amused by the misnomer and told me later that local politicians had once redbaited him when he was a candidate for the U.S. Congress.

The Federal Bureau of Investigation was concerned that our center, liberated from the new fur traders, had become a nest of subversive radicals and communists. Federal agencies monitored our telephones, and there was at least one double agent at the center. The mole, a native employment counselor, was exposed by an easy deception. I mentioned in a telephone conversation a strategic, executive session at the center and then waited to see who would respond to the bait. The mole was there on time. He was convinced that communists were a serious threat to native cultures, and then pleaded not to reveal his name.

Louise McCannel, director of the Walker Foundation, and her husband, Malcolm, an eye surgeon, were the first to grant money to the new native service center. They responded to a newspaper story about my objectives. Ronald Libertus arrived on the same day and contributed the cost of salaries for one month. The money, received as a loan, was returned several months later. The political and literary sovereignty of the center might not have been possible without their trust and generosity. Libertus was later elected to serve on the board of directors.

Seven of the survivance narratives in this book are based on my personal experiences as director of the center. Rattling Hail, Roman Downwind, Marleen American Horse, Laurel Hole In The Day, and Baptiste Saint Simon are real natives with protective fictional names. Their stories convey the adversity, courage, and irony of native survivance and literary sovereignty.

Zebulon Matchi Makwa, the memorable Mother Earth Man, was loved by blond women and thousands of black flies. The names conceal his actual identity. Colonel Whitehall, the superintendent of a federal boarding school, Girlie Blahswomann, the mixed-blood prom queen turned Kundalini Yogi, Farlie Border, and Beacher and Daisie Givens are fictitious names for real characters.

Clement Beaulieu is my pseudonym, a communal association with my native family. I borrowed these two names, a literary disposition, to represent my actual presence as a character in several scenes and stories. The pseudonym eschews the burdens and restrictions of the first person grammatical category. Beaulieu is the birth name of my paternal grandmother, Alice Beaulieu Vizenor. These two surnames are associated with the early fur trade in the Great Lakes. Clement is the second name of my great uncle, John Clement Beaulieu, and the first name of my father. My grandmother, great uncle, and father were born on the White Earth Reservation in Minnesota.

Personal and historical names are the sources and manner of distinctive identities. Native traditions are created and endure in stories. Nature is a union, not a separation, and personal identities are visionary. Fiction, dreams, imitations, and the politics of names are at once partitioned and not separable. The name "Indian," for instance, is a simulation with no actual reference. The American Indian, likewise, is the tricky trace of an absence. Natives are a presence, and the stories that arise in singular native languages are an absolute reference in time, place, and memory. Names are both burdens and literary sovereignty.

An unforgettable man and woman arrived late on a summer day almost forty years ago at the American Indian Employment Center on Franklin Avenue in Minneapolis. I was tired, distracted by the extreme politics of community service, and eager to leave for a weekend in northern Minnesota. The couple entered my office and sat in overstuffed upholstered chairs near my desk.

The man was a mixed-blood native with bright blue eyes. His face and hands were weathered, marked by scars, and he seemed to bear an enormous sense of personal disaster. The native woman wore an oversized shirt that was stained, smeared by vomit. She was drunk, undernourished, ancient from abuse, and when she moved her mouth to speak, the creases on her face sagged under an enormous cultural burden. The fetid odor of her slow breath and the vomit on her clothes permeated the office. The man blamed racialism and the dominant culture for his problems, and that included alcoholism, the moment, motive, and mark of poverty. Adversely, he seemed to be secure in the tragic summons of victimry.

I was not in the mood at the end of the week to listen to mundane racial stories about white demons in the city. Native shamans on the reservation were more treacherous. I told him in a rather nasty tone of voice that some shaman might take back his native blood one night and that would solve his many problems.

"You need white people, more than they need you now to blame for your problems, your personal problems." He was silent and turned away, partly because he was subservient to the services provided by the center. My tone of voice was severe but carried little conviction. "You need them to keep you the way you are so you can moan in self pity, but pity is a bad tongue for tribal apostates."

The native woman raised her head and slowly looked around the room. Conference posters were tacked to the walls, including an enlarged image of Chief Joseph by the photographer Edward Curtis. The woman smiled and then, standing near the desk, she motioned toward the door with her chin and lips, in a tribal manner. "Stand now, the flag is coming through the door." She must have seen the traditional ceremonial tribal staff of eagle feathers in a vision. She raised her hands, gestured toward the door, and sang a native song, an honoring song, over the frightful protests of her man. Tears trailed down the creases on her cheeks. Somehow, by her honoring song, she became sober, her eyes were clear, and then she reached toward me with her small hands. "It feels so good to just talk again," she said in a gentle voice, almost a whisper. She touched my hand. That song was a survivance story. She had, by her visionary presence, turned the burdens of racialism and poverty into a moment of literary sovereignty.

Native stories are "imaginative and creative in nature. It is an act by which man strives to realize his capacity for wonder, meaning, and delight," observed N. Scott Momaday at the First Convocation of American Indian Scholars. "It is also a process in which man invests and preserves himself in the context of ideas. Man tells stories in order to understand his experience, whatever it may be. The possibilities of storytelling are precisely those of understanding the human experience."

Reverend George Smith, the native vicar of the Episcopal Church in Cass Lake, Minnesota, assured me that the older native women in his parish would soon return to his services. Alas, most of the senior women had defected to the Church of Jesus Christ of the Latter-day Saints. The Mormons had built a new church that summer, some forty years ago, and the callow young missionaries were active in native communities on the Leech Lake Reservation.

George served traditional *anishinaabe* corn soup after his service, and that brought me closer to monotheism than any promises of salvation. I was encamped in the Chippewa National Forest that summer working on a book of original haiku. Sunday services were decidedly senior and communal by gesture and memory. The older women were curiously shy but never wary, a generous, native tease of charity and shared stories.

Then, out of the blue, the older native widows turned their backs on the reservation episcopate, smiled without reserve, and attended the new Mormon Church.

Earlier that summer the missionaries were determined to somehow convert the seniors by obligation, but they were always outwitted by native reciprocity. The young men, dressed in their dark, bargain suits and uneven ties, awkwardly worked the long line on humid nights at the local Dairy Queen. The old widows, in an equitable and proper trade for transportation to the market or the public health hospital, baked fresh berry pies for the missionaries.

The Mormon Church, later that summer, launched a splendid, if not desperate, program of free false teeth for any native elder who participated in services. The older women could not resist the chance to wear a new, toothy smile, but in turn they devised an original measure of reciprocity.

"No need to worry," said George Smith. "They'll return as soon as they decide the fair trade of church services for a set of false teeth, and then they'll be back with new smiles and stories." Five to seven weeks of attendance was the touchstone measure of denture reciprocity. The seniors returned to the reservation episcopate, and the memorable stories of that summer are native traces of survivance and literary sovereignty.

The last four stories in this edition are about people who were directly related or regrettably connected in some way to Thomas James White Hawk, a handsome, moody, tragic premedical student at the University of South Dakota in Vermillion.

White Hawk was sentenced to death by electrocution for the murder of James Yeado, a respected, amiable senior jeweler in the college town, and for the brutal rape of his wife, Dorthea, on March 24, 1967. White Hawk "was found in the Yeado home, and did not resist arrest," reported the *Vermillion Plain Talk*. "Authorities were reluctant to divulge information on what happened in the Yeado home on Good Friday." James Yeado had been shot, beaten on the head, and bound in a braided rug.

Douglas Hiza, the vicar of the Episcopal Church in Vermillion, reported that White Hawk called him from the Yeado home on Good Friday. Hiza, who regularly visited White Hawk in the Clay County jail, said that he described a gruesome, demonic ritual on Good Friday. White Hawk collected blood from the dead man and baked it in the oven.

Circuit judge James Bandy imposed the death sentence on January 15, 1968. "It is the sentence and judgment of this Court, and it is ordered and adjudged, that, by reason of your conviction of the crime of murder of James Yeado, you, Thomas James White Hawk, suffer death by electrocution, and may God have mercy upon your soul." White Hawk was convicted and sentenced to death without a trial because the proceedings had ended when he changed his plea to guilty.

South Dakota once banned the death penalty, between 1915 and 1939. Thirteen men, including several natives, have been executed by court order in the state. Jack McCall was the first recorded execution in 1877. He was hanged for shooting Wild Bill Hickok in Deadwood, South Dakota, according to information provided by the South Dakota Department of Corrections.

Brave Bear was the first native legally executed in South Dakota. He was hanged in 1882 for "the murder of a pioneer settler." Chief Two Sticks was hanged in 1894 for "instigating the slaying of three cowboys." Ernest Loveswar was hanged in 1902 for "the murder of two homesteaders," and that same year George Bear was hanged for murder. George Sitts was the last person executed in South Dakota. He was electrocuted in 1947 for the murders of two state criminal agents.

The *Minneapolis Tribune* published a report on the death sentence in January 1968. White Hawk was pictured in uniform as a student at the Shattuck School in Faribault, Minnesota. That concise account of the crime, and of his life as an orphan, changed my life for the next two years. I put aside my work on a novel and a few days later drove to South Dakota with Ronald Libertus. We learned that natives there were not eager to oppose capital punishment in the name of Thomas White Hawk. His crimes had brought shame to natives in the state.

I traveled in South Dakota for more than six months and interviewed more than a hundred individuals, including public officials and those natives and teachers who knew White Hawk and his family. My critical research on the case was published a year later. Louise McCannel funded the production and distribution of several thousand copies of *Thomas James White Hawk*. My forty-page quarto brochure was read by an active international audience. South Dakota was viewed by serious activists as one of the most racist states in the country. I was a board member at the time of the Minnesota American Civil Liberties Union.

Joseph Satten, a psychiatrist at the Menninger Clinic in Topeka, Kansas, reported that White Hawk suffered from psychotic episodes and lapsed into "transient" dreams. "His Indian background would tend to make him place a high value on stoicism, emotional impassivity, withdrawal, aloofness, and the denial of dependence on others. In addition, the tendency of some in the dominant culture to devalue Indians and the Indian culture would tend to accentuate his feelings of loneliness and suspicion." Satten romanced the obvious simulations of natives, and at the same time, he supported my idea of "cultural schizophrenia."

Governor Frank Farrar of South Dakota commuted the death sentence imposed on White Hawk. "While I favor the retention of the capital punishment laws on the books for whatever deterrent value and use in future cases they might have, the imposition of a life sentence can be punishment equally as severe to the defendant as the death penalty," he announced at a press conference on October 24, 1969. The governor personally requested that future petitions to commutate his sentence be denied by the parole board. "Having to live and face daily the inhumane act may be for the defendant as great a punishment as death itself."

The South Dakota Board of Pardons and Paroles reported to the governor that no further commutations would be made. White Hawk, without the possibility of parole, faced a natural death sentence in the state penitentiary.

I last visited White Hawk with his lawyer, Douglas Hall, at the state penitentiary in June 1987. I had not seen White Hawk for twenty years, not since the trial of his accomplice William Stands and at the parole board hearing to appeal his death sentence. He was moody, distracted by other visitors, and evasive about a parole petition in his name. White Hawk never expressed remorse for the crimes he committed, and he never overtly demonstrated a mature sense of the sorrow and shame he caused in the native community.

"The same sharp emotions that made headlines in the late 1960s will surface again next month when confessed murderer Thomas White Hawk, a Minnesota-educated American Indian, requests that his life sentence be commuted to allow him the possibility of parole," wrote Dan Oberdorfer for the *Minneapolis Star Tribune* on August 3, 1987. Hall "acknowledges that he has a tough job ahead of him. He has notified the South Dakota Board of Pardons and Paroles of his intention to seek to have White Hawk's sentence commuted."

White Hawk was an active participant in the Native American Church. That, however, was not seen as reason to consider parole. He was popular in the penitentiary, a trusted inmate, but the sense of rage about his crimes would not be forgiven by parole.

Thank you "for the good visits and for the support during our forthcoming fight. I can foresee quite a bit of trouble along the way because of the mental illness issue though. Let's just hope things won't be too tough," White Hawk wrote Hall on May 10, 1987.

"I have done some heavy thinking and I have been unable to come up with any feasible method for altering Gerald Vizenor's journal to suit our purposes now," White Hawk wrote Hall. "Vizenor's work was superbly written and the only elements which I believe we could alter at all would be the placement of the transcript quotes he used. Otherwise, I would change nothing."

Thomas James White Hawk died of a heart attack at the state penitentiary on May 7, 1997. He was forty-nine years old, and he had been in prison for thirty years. "Dying was probably the only way he was ever going to get out," wrote Doug Grow for the *Star Tribune*.

White Hawk was constrained and deceived by his own prosaic narcissism, arrogance, and vanity. His best moments were poses, or simulations of a presence; otherwise he was moody. He was elusive and evasive, but these were strategies not debilities; his poses were at times masterly, and yet he was, to a fault, responsive to authority. He wrote hundreds of pages of notes and philosophical ideas when he was detained, a teenage rapist and murderer, in the Clay County Jail in Vermillion, South Dakota.

"Many contemporary people raise the question: How can one both behave in an unrestrained way and at the same time believe correctly that such behavior is wrong? Some people deny that it is possible to do this knowingly," he wrote in the summer of 1967.

As Socrates thought, it is monstrous, at a time when knowledge is actually present, for anything else to be in charge, dragging knowledge around like a slave. Socrates used to argue wholeheartedly against such a view, his idea being that there is no such thing as lack of restraint, since no one could or would knowingly act contrary to the good. That could only happen through ignorance.

This theory is obviously at variance with plain fact. We must examine the failing more closely, and see if it happens through ignorance—what sort of ignorance this is!

It is clear that the unrestrained man does not think it right to do what he does until he is actually "out of control."

Some thinkers allow part of this, but not all of it. They agree with the view that nothing can be superior to knowledge; but not with the view that no one acts contrary to what, in his opinion, is the best. For this reason they say that the unrestrained man, when he comes under the influence of pleasures, does not have knowledge; he has opinions instead. But if it is opinion, and not knowledge, and if the opposing idea is not strong, but weak (as happens with people who are of two minds), it is an understandable fault to stick to such ideas in the face of powerful desires.

CONTENTS

Wordarrows

Separatists and Urban Fur Traders

SEPARATISTS
BEHIND THE BLINDS

The Bureau of Indian Affairs has been wished dead more times than evil, but colonial evil is better outwitted than dead because someone would be sure to create a more depraved form of tribal control.

One of the oldest colonial bureaus in the federal government, planned first under the War Department and later transferred to the division of Land Management in the Department of the Interior, revealing federal ambivalence toward tribal people, has survived all death wishes like pale cockroaches from the old cities.

The Bureau of Indian Affairs continues to feed on linear words from field reports, swelling on white paper, indifferent research, while children hunger down five generations of tribal memories.

No one is alive now who remembers from personal experience the vernal morning when the cedar still stood and the rivers were wild and clean; the good time before the federal government created tribal exclaves through treaties and appointed tactical separatists, colonial administrators, to exploit native people and their resources.

What the federal government has done to native tribes with humor-less trickeries and faithless promises should never be forgotten.

Thousands of tribal people moved from reservations to urban centers, meaning to leave behind evil, their hunger and grim mem-ories, but the federal colonialists were waiting like the cockroaches to define tribal places in the cities. The sons and daughters of those who had first settled on urban reservations demanded programs and services to change the limits of their lives.

The time was spring in the middle sixties. The place, in the morn-ing, was the Edward Waite Neighborhood House on Park Avenue in Minneapolis, and in the afternoon, the Minneapolis Area Office of the Bureau of Indian Affairs located on Lake Street. The event was the first organized protest against the federal colonialists. The par-ticipants were tribal children, the unemployed, several high school dropouts, old tribal people with walking sticks, college students, drinkers and wanderers from the streets, and one white lawyer, who marched in the picket line in his suit and conservative tie.

"When we hit the lines leave these plain brown sacks of cock-roaches in the federal buildings. . . . We will be moving in a few minutes," said Clement Beaulieu to the tribal people waiting in the garage behind the Neighborhood House.

Clement Beaulieu was a tribal advocate on the urban reservation. He organized, with the assistance of George Mitchell, Mary Thunder, and several others, the Urban American Indian Protest Committee and the first national protest, demanding that the Bureau of Indian Affairs offer services to tribal people in the cities. "The urban reser-vation is the largest in the state," said the advocate, "and tribal people should be served wherever they live."

Protests and picket lines were new experiences on the urban reservation, and some were opposed to demonstrations. Dennis Banks, for one, before his radical transformation as one of the political and spiritual leaders of the American Indian Movement, when his hair was cut short, martial short, and he wore summer suits with white shirts and ties, said that "demonstrations are not the Indian way."

Banks was right, but not for the right reasons. Holding a sign bearing protest bromides was not a traditional tribal experience for either clowns or warriors, but because it was immature, simple-minded, and embarrassing to proud people, white urbanites understood the messages and supported the event. Picketing was not tribal, but it was the language of white natives stuck on television in the suburbs. Banks, who in the middle sixties avoided demonstrations and protest rhetoric, later learned the power of televised bromides. Conservative as he seemed then, his views were shared by most tribal people, which made the organization of a demonstration a double challenge.

Beaulieu, determined to state the troubles of urban tribal people through demonstrations and other means, called upon his friends and relatives for assistance. Some served as drivers to transport tribal people to and from the demonstration site at the area office, and others printed bromides and messages and fixed them to sticks. It was a good time, people were not without fear, but the memories have lasted and those who were there live with a certain historical praise.

Beaulieu asked Mary Thunder to find as many tribal children as she could lead on the picket line. She walked into several elementary school classrooms, interrupted the teachers, and left with all the tribal children. She was also responsible for encouraging other tribal mothers to participate, which was important then because the slogan for the demonstration was "AIM AGAINST BIAS," "American Indian mothers against the Bureau of Indian Affairs' stupidity."

Late in the morning there were nineteen tribal people, most of them children, waiting in the garage behind the Neighborhood House. The people played pool and ate rolls while they waited for the first protest to begin. Dozens of tribal people who promised to to be at the protest did not appear or call in their regrets. At the last minute, before the protest began, Beaulieu drove through the urban reservation looking for tribal people on the streets. When he found an individual, or a couple, he promised free dinners and a place in tribal histories for demonstrating their feelings against colonialism and federal separatists. Thirteen strangers picked up on the streets participated in the protest.

When the drivers lined up their cars waiting to transport the tribal protesters to the area office, the receptionist at the Neighborhood House told Beaulieu that a man named Gus Hall was waiting outside for permission to join the demonstration. Gus Hall was the general secretary of the Communist Party in America.

"Gus Hall, are you certain he said his name was Gus Hall?" Beaulieu asked the receptionist. She said she was certain that was his name.

"Gus Hall is a Communist," said Beaulieu.

"Who cares?" said the receptionist.

"Senator Humphrey, and television and the newspapers will too, . . . not to mention the rednecks and racists on the prairie," said Beaulieu. "Tell him to wait, tell him to wait a few minutes for me."

Beaulieu closed his office door and looked out the window while he considered the consequences of permitting the general secretary of the Communist Party in America to participate in the first demonstration against the Bureau of Indian Affairs. The movement would be associated with communism and unpatriotism. Gus Hall was free from federal restrictions and had mellowed with time, but politicians and old union members would not forget his brash management of the Young Communist League in Minnesota and his condemnation of capitalism when he was arrested during the Minneapolis Teamsters strike. The nation would side with the federal government and not with tribal people if a communist leader were seen at the demonstration. But would television and newspapers report the protest? A communist on the line would make it news, national and international news. Gus Hall in a new war dance. Gus Hall adds the tomahawk to the hammer and sickle. Gus Hall would make the protest news and then, once the issues were in the news, the protest committee could exclude and dispossess communism.

"Mister Hall," said Beaulieu, introducing himself. "This is a pleasure. . . . We will be leaving for the area office in a few minutes and we would be pleased to have you march with us this afternoon."

Hall smoked a pipe and was dressed in a tweed suit coat. He wore plastic-framed spectacles. He looked down when he spoke and when he listened, showing his bald head, and glanced up when he paused between sentences. He was slow to answer questions, gesturing with gentle hand movements. His pipe tobacco smelled foul.

Beaulieu pinched his nose and smiled.

"Douglas Hall, there, it is you," exclaimed Archie Goldman, executive director of the Waite Neighborhood House, as he came around the corner of the building. Douglas Hall is a lawyer who has been active in labor organizations—too active for some conservative managers—and human rights movements, and persuasive in liberal politics. "Douglas, you *are* looking good, trim there at the waist, and how is your wife? Listen, are you here for the beginning of this incredible revolution?"

"Yes, as one of the demonstrators," said Hall.

"Goldman told me you were Gus Hall," said Beaulieu.

"Never, forked tongue talk," said Goldman.

"Goldman speaks with ease now," said Beaulieu, "but wait until tomorrow when his board learns that the revolution was started in the garage."

"Listen, this is a good thing," said Goldman, huffing and puffing too hard on his pipe. He was enveloped in his own smoke.

"So much for communism," said Beaulieu.

Beaulieu did not issue the protest signs until the tribal people were at the area office. The children were eager to hold signs and march in front of the government windows, but the older tribal people, those on walking sticks, the elders with grim memories from the federal boarding schools, were hesitant and embarrassed to be seen in a protest demonstration. The elders had not forgotten the power of the colonial separatists. Most of the demonstrators were uncomfortable until three white men in a red car passed the picketers several times, shouting "go back to the reservation . . . dirt and savages never work . . . get your asses off welfare . . . savages suck . . . you got enough hands out now."

The tribal children stuck out their tongues and waved their signs like crosses at the passing white men. The signs had several misspelled words. One misspelled word, proglem for problem, was given meaning in print. The definition of a proglem (combining the meaning of problem and program) is that which is rendered from federal programs designed to solve people problems from a distance. The signs were printed in black and brown and red ink: No More Apologies . . . Negotiate Don't Dictate . . . We Don't Want to Return to Reservations . . . Stop Studying the Indian Problem—The Bureau of Indian Affairs Is Not under the War Department Anymore . . . Serve Indians Not Lands . . . Give Us Jobs and Training Not Commodities . . . The Bureau of Indian Affairs Can't Get Along without Us Now.

The demonstrators were given facts about the Bureau of Indian Affairs and instructed how to respond to questions about the purposes of the demonstration. The tribal protesters were told to express their emotions first and then the critical facts. White federal officials had no position from which to debate emotional statements.

George Mitchell and Mary Thunder prepared a two-page statement which was distributed during the demonstration. The statement listed the annual budget and the total number of employees in the Bureau of Indian Affairs. Other information was critical of federal services.

"One-third of the total Indian population in Minnesota lives in urban centers. Therefore, the Urban American Indians demand that the Bureau of Indian Affairs direct one-third of its programs to the Urban Center Indians in this area.

"We do not want to live in the depressed reservation areas. We want to live and work in normal American urban communities, but the Bureau of Indian Affairs will not serve the needs of the Indian unless he is somehow identified with reservation Indian trust lands, living in rural poverty.

"We want to be served like humans and not like quantities of land. We are Indians, that should be enough to be served by the Bureau of Indian Affairs.

"We wonder what the Irish, the Swedes, or the American Negro would have to say about a Bureau of Irish Affairs, a Bureau of Swedish Affairs, or a Bureau of Negro Affairs, which did not serve the needs of urban citizens.

"The Bureau of Indian Affairs does more for land, roads, and trees, than it does for Indian people. We demand that the Bureau of Indian Affairs negotiate not dicate.

"These are the things we demand:

"Assistance in orientation to city life . . .

"Assistance in finding housing . . .

"Assistance in using legal and medical facilities . . .

"Assistance in forming and developing effective Indian community organizations representing urban Indian interests and needs.

"Job training and education in *this* area, not in another part of the country. We don't want to be relocated. We like it here and we would like to be trained, live, and work in this area.

"Assistance in finding and adjusting to employment . . .

"The Bureau of Indian Affairs should send their employees into the community where the Indians live, to understand the urban Indian needs. There have been enough studies and statistics about the Indian. We are tired of being talked about, it's time for the Bureau of Indian Affairs to get to work."

The demands were not unusual, the need for services to urban tribal people had been established in simple emotions at the demonstration, but demanding that a portion of federal funds allocated to the tribes be redirected to urban centers was not a popular view on reservations. Elected tribal leaders had their own problems on the reservations and could not support urban diversions. Tribal politicians were in tacit agreement with the Bureau of Indian Affairs.

Clement Beaulieu wrote to Robert Bennett, then Commissioner of Indian Affairs, about the problems of tribal people being denied services in urban centers.

"I have your letter," Bennett responded in a letter, "relating to the picketing of the Area Office of the Bureau of Indian Affairs in Minneapolis as a protest of the discontent by Indian people with the Bureau's inability to work on urban Indian problems.

"I am sure that you and many other Indian people feel that you should not be dependent upon the Bureau of Indian Affairs for services, particularly when you have established residence in cities throughout the country. I know that you would not want the Bureau of Indian Affairs to follow Indian people wherever they may go in this country but that you would rather share in the community life wherever you establish your home.

"The ability of the Bureau of Indian Affairs to provide services to Indians who have established residence away from the reservation is a matter of law as well as policy in that funds appropriated by Congress are for particular services, primarily for those on or near Indian reservations. It would seem to me that Indian people who are residents and citizens of communities and States throughout the country who have need for services should apply to the same agencies that provide services to other citizens of the community. They are certainly entitled to these services."

Glen Landbloom, then area director of the Bureau of Indian Affairs office in Minneapolis, summoned his best and smoothest tongue to invite the protest organizers into his office for a talk. "My door is always open," he said, but no one accepted his offer. "We came here to change policies not to cultivate conversations," responded Beaulieu.

Landbloom issued an order that the blinds be drawn during the picketing of the building. Notwithstanding the order, some tribal employees, like prisoners behind horizontal bars, separated the metal blinds and smiled at the demonstrators. Visiting hours had ended.

"Those bastards sit at their desks while our children are starving," said George Mitchell to Sam Newlund, staff writer for the *Minneapolis Tribune*. "Outside on the street the arrowstocracy is on the move and inside they hang around the office. . . . They're dumb on one end and numb on the other."

Robert Treuer, former labor organizer and Bureau of Indian Affairs official at the office in Bemidji, Minnesota, wrote to Beaulieu following the demonstration, that "one of these days we'll have to get together and I'll give you a cram course on social protest, direct action techniques, with particular emphasis on picketing. I'm not enamoured of the picketing stunt—it just gave the Bureau of Indian Affairs hierarchy a chance to look good with their superiors in Washington."

The demonstration was reported in newspapers and on radio and television. Liberal politicians supported the general demands of the protesters and white people rallied behind the tribal underdogs who seemed to be fighting a heroic battle against the evil federal colonialists. The demonstration was the first passionate tribal drama that served to focus some attention, however limited, on the adverse living situations of tribal people in urban centers of the dominant culture.

Several months later the Bureau of Indian Affairs announced that it would provide funding for an urban employment and social services center in Minneapolis. When the demonstration ended, people and programs changed.

Glen Landbloom was transferred from the area office to a reservation post. Mary Thunder continued working in good humor with tribal children and writing an urban reservation newsletter. George Mitchell organized an urban tribal teen center and expressed more interest in local politics. Douglas Hall, who was first introduced to tribal people on the picket lines, became active in tribal organizations as a result of the demonstration. Sam Newlund turned his attention to tribal people. His writing was balanced and accurate. Joe Rigert, then an editorial writer for the *Minneapolis Tribune*, followed news stories with sensitive editorials supporting a new tribal consciousness.

Gus Hall, Or Arvo Kusta Halberg as he was named at birth by his Finnish immigrant father when the family lived near Virginia, Minnesota, never made the demonstration at the area office of the Bureau of Indian Affairs. But several months later, following the first convention of the Communist Party in America in seven years, where Hall was elected general secretary by acclamation, he asked tribal people to write about their experiences with federal colonialism for communist newspapers.

Tribal people have a passionate attachment to their land and an unusual sense of patriotism for the nation, which bounds between love and hate, but is not without good humor. The tribal protest committee refused to write for the communists because—in addition to political reasons—there was too little humor in communist speech, making it impossible to know the hearts of the speakers.

RATTLING HAIL CEREMONIAL

Rattling Hail, he said in a harsh voice, was his whole name in all languages. He was a veteran from a recent war. For his patriotic service as an enlisted man, representing the reservation prairie tribes, he was awarded several ribbons, which he wore on the suit coat he was given at a church clothing sale, service-connected dental care, educational benefits, and, for losing one leg on a land mind, he was awarded a small pension as a disabled veteran.

Clement Beaulieu encountered Rattling Hail four times in four months as in a new urban ceremonial. When Rattling Hail visited the American Indian Employment and Guidance Center for the first time, on the first morning the center opened, he hobbled across the tile floor on one crutch with one pant leg tucked under his belt, folded and creased in a military manner. Beaulieu was moving a desk when the decorated veteran halted at the office door.

"Did you bastards open this place?"

"Not the bastards. . . ."

"Who are you?" asked Rattling Hail.

"Beaulieu is the name, and who are you?"

"Remember Rattling Hail."

"Sacred name?" asked Beaulieu, referring to the tradition of giving sacred dream names to tribal children. Missionaries and colonial government officials translated, with indifference to tribal cultures, familiar descriptive names and nicknames of tribal people as last names. Some missionaries thought that tribal descriptive names were sacred, but sacred names were seldom revealed to strangers.

In his book *The American Indian*, about tribal people on reservations at the turn of the last century, Warren Moorehead writes about the problem of familiar names entered on official tribal rolls. "Many years ago the employees at White Earth Agency made a roll of the Chippewa Indians. One would suppose that so important a document as a register of all the Indians would be accurate. But the original roll, as on file at the White Earth office . . . bristled with inaccuracies. For instance, the name Mah-geed is the Ojibwa pronunciation of Maggie. Many of the Indian girls were named Mah-geed by the priests and missionaries. Those who made the Government roll apparently thought that Mah-geed was a distinguished Indian name, so they entered up quite a number of Mah-geeds. No other name is added.

"The Ojibwa name for old woman is Min-de-moi-yen. To the clerks who made the roll this sounded like the name of an Indian, so they solemnly set down many such names. . . . Having assembled as our witnesses the most reliable old Indians, we were able to check up the many errors in the Government roll. Frequently there would be as many as forty or fifty Ojibwa assembled in the schoolroom where our hearings were held. When the interpreter called out such a name as Min-de-moi-yen . . . or Mah-geed, the other Indians would shout with laughter, and when they recovered sufficiently they would state they did not know what individual Indian was named as there were a score who might respond to that appellation."

Rattling Hail waited at the door.

"Or is your name a translation?" asked Beaulieu.

"Rattling Hail is Rattling Hail," said Rattling Hail, stressing over and over, with his lips drawn tight over his teeth, the word *hail*. "Rattling Hail is the whole name, all the name, that sound is me here, in all languages and tongues for all times. . . . Remember Rattling Hail."

"Standing Rock in North Dakota?" asked Beaulieu. He was interested in locating his name on a reservation, the place for the name. Where one comes from is a cultural signature, a special sign, in casual tribal diction. Some reservations have had little contact with outsiders while others, the White Earth Reservation for example, about which Warren Moorehead writes, have been virtual bicultural centers for intermarriage and cultural diffusion. Some reservations have mixedblood roots to black and white, social and genetic evidence that black soldiers and white traders did more with the tribes than contain them on colonial exclaves. Mixedbloods who hate white and black must hate that place and time in themselves.

"No reservation on me . . . no mixedblood should ask me about that," said Rattling Hail, grinding his teeth together. "What are you white bloods doing here, what is this place?"

"We are setting up an employment and social services center, a new idea for urban centers for tribal people," Beaulieu explained. "You, believe it or not, are the first person through the door. . . . We moved the desks in this morning."

"Fucking liars. . . ."

"Tell me about it," said Beaulieu.

Rattling Hail raised his crutch and hobbled around the desk toward Beaulieu. His lips spread, like a cornered animal with no escape distance, exposing his clean white perfect teeth. Check out the teeth, Beaulieu once told his friends, because perfect teeth in a tribal mouth means a government child or dental care in a foster home. Most poor people have poor teeth to prove it.

"Down with the crutch general," said Beaulieu, moving counter clockwise around the room and keeping the desk between them. "We opened the doors this morning and here you are, the first one in the door. . . . What is it you want here? Work, or a little abusement?"

"Fucking liars . . ." he said again and again. He hobbled around and around the desk swinging one crutch. "No one ever helped us with nothing. . . . Fucking liars."

"Now, look general, put down the crutch and walk out of here the same way you came in, this is not a good way to start anything," said Beaulieu. He stopped near the door to the office and waited. "This is no morning watering hole or abusement park and no one needs you here to blame the world. . . . Come back again when you are sober."

Rattling Hail lowered his crutch and hobbled toward the door. He stopped at attention in front of Beaulieu, face to face, staring from his interior darkness and grinding his perfect teeth together. Then he turned and hobbled from the building on a warm morning late in summer.

Rattling Hail appeared the second time while he was exercising his new service-connected plastic limb. He was marching, tapping at the cement with his new cane, down Vineland Place past the Walker Art Center and the Guthrie Theatre in Minneapolis. Near the entrance to the theater he stopped on the sidewalk, tapped his cane one final time, and then raised his arm and saluted with his left hand, the wrong hand, several actors and actresses leaving the building. His teeth flashed under the street lamp when he turned in a military manner, lowered his arm, and continued walking on his plastic leg.

Rattling Hail, the warrior on one leg, wounded in the white wars, saluted the theater, places in make-believe. He saluted the blond children dressed in purple tapestries—back from building imaginative castles with sacred cedar and barricades on stage with reservation plans—with the wrong hand. He must have heard the new world rehearsing overscreams from Sand Creek where Colonel John Chivington said "I have come to kill Indians, and believe it is right and honorable to use any means." He saluted the voices imitating five hundred dead at Mystic River in Connecticut, millions dead in the path of white progress.

Rattling Hail listened as he passed, he must have heard old tribal voices from the mountains and from the woodland and from the prairie. His salute was a powerful message.

Black Hawk tells that the "white men are bad schoolmasters. They carry false looks and deal in false actions. . . . The white men do not scalp the head, they do worse. They poison the heart. It is not pure with them."

Chief Joseph tells that "good words will not give my people good health and stop them from dying. . . . I am tired of talk that comes to nothing. It makes my heart sick when I remember all the good words and all the broken promises. There has been too much talking by men who had no right to talk."

Yellow Robe tells that the "coming of the white man is no different for us than dissension, cruelty, or loneliness. It is a learning for us."

Kicking Bird tells that he is a "stone, broken and thrown away. One part thrown this way and one part thrown that way. I am grieved at the ruin of my people; they will go back to the old road and I must follow them. They will not let me live with the white people."

Tribal people were hanged then, children were starved with their heads shaved. Tribal women were dismembered for souvenirs and the earth turned to crust and the water rushed through the stumps. Buffalo skulls and tree phantoms screamed on the wind.

Rattling Hail disappeared in the darkness.

When the theater rehearsals were over the actors and actresses mounted their wheels for new parties under blood-soaked beams in the urban hills. Rattling Hail had saluted their passing while other tribes enacted their cultural suicides downtown on the reservations.

Rattling Hail appeared the third time, as in a new urban ceremonial, standing behind a park bench watching the ducks feed in the autumn on the shores of the pond in Loring Park near downtown Minneapolis. He flashed his teeth, moved toward the birds, and then lifted his face and arms in flight.

Rattling Hail appeared the last time walking through the new snow without his cane. Four months from the time he first hobbled into the American Indian Employment and Guidance Center, which was moved from the northside to a corner storefront location more convenient to tribal people on Chicago Avenue near Franklin in Minneapolis, he was walking with ease on a new leg.

Clement Beaulieu was watching the first winter snow from the storefront center with several friends and volunteers who worked at the center. Night fell with the fresh snow while they talked in the growing darkness about the problems tribal people encounter in urban centers. The urban reservation was no better than colonial reservations for services, and the heartless federal government passed tribal people back and forth like crippled beasts of burden. Their work at the center was thankless and their critics were increasing in numbers because, while people were assisted with their social problems they were told to change, to give up their adjustment to poor living conditions. Tribal people were not pleased with too much change. Hostilities also grew from those who were envious of the appearance of political and economic power at the center.

The Last Lecture, a tribal watering hole for broken warriors, was located catercorner from the center on Chicago Avenue. The corner door opened at the bar and out stepped Rattling Hail, unbroken, on his new tribal flesh-tone plastic leg. He stood at attention for a few minutes on the corner, marking his place on the fantastic battle line, his perfect teeth flashing across the street through the falling snow, and then he began marching without a cane into battle toward the center.

Beaulieu and his friends were sitting inside the darkness watching Rattling Hail walk toward them. He passed beneath the street light, marching in a straight line across the street, leaving distinctive footprints. The heel on his plastic leg skimmed over the fresh snow.

Rattling Hail opened the front door of the center without hesitation, stepped inside, shook the snow from his coat, and spread his lips like an animal, flashing his teeth. The illumination in the room came through the windows from the street light outside.

Then, in silence, Rattling Hail faced each person in the storefront, as if he were an officer inspecting his troops on the line. He stared at them, his black eyes rolling from an interior darkness, rolling under tribal secrets, ground his teeth together, and then he marched out of the building without closing the door. No words were spoken. Rattling Hail, wagging his elbows in the manner of a trickster, disappeared in the snow. The new urban ceremonial had ended.

FACTORS IN
THE URBAN FUR TRADE

To most tribal people the American Indian Employment and Guidance Center was a success, but the white factors on the board, those who had founded the nonprofit service corporation, were critical of the director for being too active.

Difficult as it was to believe then, the white critics, and several tribal people, wanted to punish the director for being too assertive in placing hundreds of tribal people in work at high salaries and for organizing other urban reservation programs. The factors in the white fur trade seemed to expect the director to be passive in the operation of the center.

Reverend Raymond Baines, chairman of the center board of directors and director of the United Church Committee on Indian Work, called a secret meeting of certain board members who were critical of the director. Those attending the secret meeting discussed the behavior of the director and proposed policies to limit his activities on the urban reservation.

The division between board members was more than race and flesh tones. The differences at the board meetings were expressed in religion and political values, accents and dialects, education and social status. The director was neither passive nor intimidated by the manners of the white factors in the urban fur trade.

The more conservative members of the board and those who had attended the secret meeting seemed to value proper manners over demands and confrontations for changes in the institutions serving tribal people. The radical and more liberal members of the board cheered the director when he challenged institutional authorities and questioned the incompetence and insensitivities of the Bureau of Indian Affairs, while the conservative members of the board, who seemed embarrassed when the director made demands, expressed their fear that the funds would be terminated over disagreements. Manners were important to the conservatives.

"Those fools must slop their food over linen napkins," said Peter Vezina. "They must think this revolution is a matter of public relations, or something."

The participants at the secret meeting prepared a statement which was presented at the next board of directors meeting. The statement demanded, and not in the calm manners the conservatives seemed to honor over confrontations, that the director withdraw from all activities outside the responsibilities of the center. His accomplishments in finding work for tribal people and his administrative competence were praised, but his other activities on the urban reservation were in conflict with the expectations of the conservative members of the board.

Political involvements troubled the conservatives the most. George Mitchell entered the aldermanic primaries, opposing sixth ward incumbent Jens Christensen, who had served one term on the Minneapolis City Council, and Clement Beaulieu was named then in a newspaper article as the campaign manager for the tribal candidate. Beaulieu and Mitchell were good friends, they had planned numerous political strategies together, but those who knew Mitchell, the rugged individualist, knew that he could not be managed and did not take the news report past humor. But some of the white factors thought it was improper that the director of the center was named a manager for a political candidate.

"It would be folly to suggest that Mitchell, a one-time rodeo bronco-buster and lasso artist, is favored to survive the primary," wrote Sam Newlund in an article published in the *Minneapolis Tribune*.

"But winning isn't that important to him. The main thing, as he and his supporters describe it, is to awaken the white community to the notion that urban Indians are breathing humans with problems. . . .

"Another goal is to get Indians involved, in greater numbers than at present, in trying to change things—at the polls in this case," wrote Newlund.

Mitchell was running as a tribal candidate in the sixth ward which was situated on the urban reservation. He lost in the primary election, but the worst defeat was that few tribal people took the time to register or vote, in spite of an extensive effort to register tribal voters in the ward.

Next, the conservative members of the board criticized the director for organizing, with George Mitchell and Ronald Libertus, the first convention of urban tribal people in the nation. More than a dozen tribal people and public officials spoke at the convention, which was held in Minneapolis, including Douglas Hall, lawyer and member of the center board of directors, who set the tone for the convention. He suggested political activism on the urban reservation.

"The white man isn't going to give you anything; you are going to have to organize and take it," Hall told the audience of more than two hundred, according to an article written by Bernie Shellum and published in the *Minneapolis Tribune*.

"Get politically active—register—discuss candidates—then vote in the city elections. Make the politicians listen to the Indian community," said Hall.

The conservative members of the center board were critical also that the director was named chairman of the Mayor's Indian American Task Force. Arthur Naftalin, then mayor of Minneapolis, named Beaulieu chairman of this new task force to meet with public officials and to recommend new programs to improve services on the urban reservation. Beaulieu organized meetings with tribal people and elected public officials, members of welfare and social service boards, various commissions, and police officials. During the course of these meetings some white factors thought the appointment and the meetings served partisan political ends.

Bound to conservative rituals and manners, some conservatives on the board could not see through their partisan political templates to understand the needs of the poor. The worst of the white factors were obsessed with political polarities and potential communist conspiracies.

Chairman Baines reported at a board meeting that the director must withdraw from all political involvement, nothing less than being desk-bound on the urban reservation.

Ronald Libertus argued that the restrictions recommended by the chairman were so "binding that the director would not even be able to vote. The Central Intelligence Agency is not even this binding with undercover agents."

The discussion continued.

Samuel Scheiner: Part of his job is to remain politically neutral. He cannot be a political campaign manager. You can bury this organization if you allow your executive director to engage in politics.

Douglas Hall: But he has been involved in community awareness. I see his activities as a direct part of his responsibilities to the center. In addition to finding jobs for people he must be successful in activating the Indian Community. This will be a great mistake to limit the staff at the center. He has done good work on the task force.

Reverend Baines: We are concerned how the Bureau of Indian Affairs is looking at us, and they are questioning us, they are concerned with the activities of the director.

Henry Allen: The board has done right to determine the policies of the staff. We've got an able executive director, but there is some apprehension from Indians, they are afraid that his activities will militate against success of the program.

Roy Bjorkman: We must have some appreciation that we were getting the wrong image due to the director's activities. The director is symbolic of the center.

The Minneapolis Star reported that about a fourth of the board members of the American Indian and Guidance Center had resigned. "Or maybe they haven't. It was that kind of meeting at the Edward F. Waite Neighborhood House. . . .

"Among those 'resigning' were the Reverend Raymond Baines, board chairman; Roy Bjorkman, one of the originators of the center, and Samuel Scheiner, another original board member.

"But Douglas Hall, another board member, suggested a motion, which was adopted, saying that everything will be held in abeyance for two weeks. Baines said today he wasn't sure whether the motion covered the board members' resignations, that of the executive director, or a set of personnel policies adopted last night.

"The factions divide roughly between the director, the staff, and some twenty Indian Board members on the one hand and the board members who operated the original center on the other. . . . The board members adopted a statement of personnel policies that would prohibit the staff from engaging in political activity or heading any other organizations. . . . The question of who had resigned is still up in the air, as is the adoption of the personnel practices statement."

At the next meeting of the board of directors, Ronald Libertus said the proposed policies were based on "false assumptions . . . the world is political and the director cannot be effective without having some political involvement."

Roy Bjorkman, one of the original members of the board and a distinguished furrier and entrepreneur, stood up to speak. He projected his voice and made dramatic hand and face gestures. Several tribal people turned to avoid his gaze. "So we don't want to stifle anybody's Americanism here, we want him to belong to a political party, we want him to participate in the activities here to build a better social society.

"I have no objection to him working on the Mayor's Committee here, because he is doing a good job I understand, that isn't going to hurt his work here. . . . Let's be perfectly honest and fair, the Bureau of Indian Affairs felt a little bit offended here, and [the director] took a little pride in it when we were interrogating him here.

"Organizing the picketing committee out there, that was one thing. I don't think that he should be involved in that if he's going to be director of the American Indian Employment Center. Now, if he wants to do those things, fine. When I hire an employee and I pay him ten thousand to do a job . . . I want him to do that job first. . . .

"We want a good image here," said Roy Bjorkman.

"White or tribal image?" asked Beaulieu.

Clement Beaulieu agreed to accept the vague new policies limiting his activities as director of the center. He agreed knowing that the policies were statements of values and manners and that no one could or would enforce them. Several months later when most of the white members of the board had resigned, the policies of political involvement were reversed by tribal members who then dominated the board of the American Indian Employment and Guidance Center.

The adversaries were outwitted for the time, but not overpowered. Manners in the end became selected acts of personal and political survival. Tricksters must learn better how to balance the forces of good and evil through humor in the urban world.

Downtown on the Reservation

ROMAN DOWNWIND

R oman Downwind was born in an abandoned station wagon on the shore of a remote lake without a name in the Chippewa National Forest during the wild-ricing season. The rice was poor that year. Roman was the fourteenth child. His mother took the rice as a cash crop. His father was in prison.

Roman moved to the urban reservation, Franklin Avenue in Minneapolis, when he was nineteen to live with his cousins. He twice failed the state driving examination. During his third effort behind the wheel he told the examination officer that he was born poor in the back seat of a car on the reservation.

"White people could at least give me a license to drive what I first took breath in. . . . No one gave me a choice," said Roman.

The officer talked about wild rice and hunting, and an arrangement was made between the two to meet in the woods during the deer hunting season, when the officer would have the good fortune of getting his deer.

Roman scored one above passing. On his way back to the urban reservation he bought three cases of cheap beer, with the last of his

money, for a celebration. He had passed his driving test and was
legal behind the wheel for the first time in eight years of driving.

Roman moved through too much urban tribal time in drunkenness. The weekend passed with beer and stories. Tuesday morning
his cousin told him he had to leave because other relatives were
coming down from the reservation. He was alone and without food
or a place to live.

Late in the afternoon he wandered into a church-supported, social-
service referral center and with his head down told the blonde volunteer social service worker about his situation. No gas, no money,
no food, in that order of importance.

"Where are you from?" the blonde asked.

"Leech Lake Reservation."

"How long have you been here?"

"Few weeks . . . no work, " he said with his head down.

"How old are you?"

"Nineteen, but . . ."

"Where have you worked before?" she asked.

"Logging on the reservation."

"Where do you live?"

"No place now," he said, shifting his feet.

"Do you have a telephone?"

"No."

"How can I reach you?"

"When?"

"Whenever we find you work," she explained.

Silence

"Do you have a car?"

"Yes"

"Then you can drive to work, at least."

"No."

"No, did you say no?"

"No, I don't have no gas."

"Do you have a license to drive?"

"Yes, yes," he said, running his hand through his black hair. His lips twitched when he spoke with pride about having passed his driving test. "Last week I passed the test on the first try. The man said I did a good job, he said I was one of the best drivers he had come through, even wanted to come up hunting and ricing with me in the fall. . . . Yes, I got a license now."

"Do you have auto insurance?" she asked.

"For what?"

"Where will you live until your first pay check?"

"No place. . . . In my car," he said smiling.

"In your car?"

"Yes, is there something wrong with that?"

"People don't sleep in their cars," she said.

"I was born there."

"Where?" she asked, looking up at him.

"In a car, something wrong with that, is there?"

"Not much work around now," she said, shuffling through the papers on her desk, "but you could try your luck downtown at the day labor pools. . . . But we take no responsibility in recommending the pools." She brushed back her blonde hair, sitting behind a huge wood desk, the top of which was covered with marble linoleum. "Not much here for someone with no experience, but we might have something in a few days, tomorrow perhaps. . . . Here is my card, you can call me at that number any time during working hours and ask for me. Not much comes in for inexperienced workers, but once in awhile we get some short term labor stuff, you may know that, loading and unloading at small factories."

"Do you know where I could get some gas?"

"No, sorry about that."

"Do you know where I could eat?"

"At a restaurant. . . . No, just joking. Roman, yes it is your name, Roman Downwind, could I call you Roman? Fine, now, well," she said with hesitation, "we could give you one or two meal passes and bus money to get to work, but the trouble is you should have a job first. . . ."

"But I am hungry now," he said.

"Let me check with the director first," said the blonde social service volunteer as she unwound her muscular legs from the legs of her chair and dialed the director on the telephone. "Charlie, this is Debbie downstairs. I have a young Indian here, just finished the intake questions, he has no experience or skills, difficult to place anywhere. Well, he needs a meal, could we put him down for one, call it work, with some bus money, enough to get downtown to unemployment?

"Ok, yes, yes, no . . . well, you know the answer to that," said the blonde volunteer worker to the director. "You know the answer to that without asking. . . . Of course, see you tonight for dinner."

Roman brushed the leg of his trousers. Waiting with his head down he focused on his shoes. He shifted his shoes on the heel and tapped his toes together, lapping and overlapping the edges of the soles, one over the other. Time takes so much time with volunteers.

"Here are two meal tickets for the diner down the street, the name of the place is right here," she said, spreading the tickets out on the desk like pets. When he reached for them she pulled back her hands not to touch him. "These tickets are good for one meal each, you can choose the meal and the time, but we suggest you choose a well balanced meal for dinner . . . and here is a voucher note for two dollars which will be given to you in cash by the bookkeeper when you leave the building."

Roman tapped his shoes again and then reached for the voucher note. He looked over at the social service worker. She was a church volunteer who wore her diamonds when she worked her two afternoons a week with the poor. When she leaned back, withdrawing her hands from the linoleum-covered desk, her breasts expanded against her blouse. Roman could see through the space between the buttons a pink flower embroidered at the center of her crisp white brassiere.

"Remember to call me now about work."

"Tomorrow for sure," he said.

"Remember that now," she said, shifting her feet.

Roman watched her blouse open and close between the buttons. When she stopped moving he looked up at her smooth short blonde hair.

"The rest is up to you now," she said, folding her arms over her breasts and covering the pink flower exposed between the buttons on her blouse. "You're a nice-looking young man, you should do better for yourself, take better care of yourself. Do you have a drinking problem?"

"No, not now," he said and then stood up to leave.

"Good for you."

Roman held out the voucher and frowned.

"Near the front door when you leave," she said, referring to the office where he could cash in the voucher. Three bracelets slid down her smooth tanned forearm to her wrist when she motioned with her hands as she spoke. For a moment Roman saw the pink flower again, but when he sat down to watch she folded her arms over her chest.

"Call me tomorrow and keep your spirits up."

Roman raised his head and looked at her face, but when she saw his dark eyes she turned away, she looked at her fingers, her bracelets, the desk, and then the telephone. He watched her face and nervous hands. He could smell her perfume. The telephone rang and she motioned him to leave the office.

Roman hit the streets again on the urban reservation. He had a beautiful white woman in his mind, two meal tickets, and enough money to buy a pack of cigarettes and enough gas to find a woman for the night. His life had meaning for one more night.

MARLEEN AMERICAN HORSE

The United States Army Corps of Engineers contracted for the construction of the Garrison Dam to hold back the Missouri River in North Dakota. Elbowoods, a small tribal village, the home and birthplace of Marleen American Horse, fell beneath the new flood, the federal creation of Lake Sakakawea, on the Fort Berthold Reservation.

Marleen American Horse came to Minneapolis with a single change of clothes in a brown paper sack and an old reservation allotment map showing her place on the earth before the flood. Not before the great mythical tribal flood which balanced the sacred earth, but before the flood of white men and their pleasure boats.

She even married a white man after the flood, a truck driver who turned violent toward women when he was drunk, which was three times a week on schedule, and he expressed his love for her on the same schedule. Three mixedblood children later, two dark and one light, and a decade since the flood, she traveled to the same bars to be with the man who abused her for her sins. She became a despondent alcoholic.

In drunkenness she gave herself to evil lust and the hostilities of white men who loved to abuse tribal women. Morning after morning, she recognized her desolation and personal destruction. Her children hungered alone at night in a cold apartment. Drinking was all she could do to ease the guilt and pain from drinking. She smiled as best she could in the late mornings with numb lips, and turned under the memories of her sacred tribal past. But she would not give up her translated tribal name.

> *she learned english*
> *without a winter coat*
> *in a cold place for sacred names*
> *milking cows*
> *on federal labor farms*
> *for another race*
> *her brown feet*
> *breaking through her red charity shoes*
> *squaw for the soldiers*
> *who bought her another drink*
> *white city soldiers*
> *cursing her dark eyes at night*
> *mauling her breasts for the cavalry*
> *without a name*
> *she was down*
> *in a civilization she never understood*
> *living forever*
> *when the soldiers fell*
> *one by one at the winter bar*
> *she raised the sacred flag of her people*
> *lifting with the eagles*
> *dreaming*
> *her children were coming home*

Marleen American Horse lost her children. Welfare workers placed them in foster homes. One winter morning when she returned from drinking, walking through the fresh snow, she learned that she had been evicted from her apartment. The locks were changed. There was an eviction notice on the door. Her television set, her clothes, memorabilia, and the reservation map showing her birthplace, the few objects remaining in her name, were gone, stolen or given away.

She slumped in the snow on the outside stairs and began to weep and wail for her children and her losses to white men and alcoholism. She wanted nothing more than to be loved in a cold and insensitive world. Her weaknesses were shunned on the street. She slipped into a telephone booth, shivering from the cold, and called a welfare worker who in turn referred her to the Waite Neighborhood House on Park Avenue in Minneapolis.

"Good morning, Waite House," said the receptionist.

"This is my last dime to call. . . ."

"Who would you like to speak to?"

"My children are gone. . . ."

"One minute please."

The call was transferred to the tribal advocate at the Neighborhood House. He was drinking coffee in the kitchen of the old mansion. He was a mixedblood writer who became an advocate for tribal people in trouble. Whatever the reason, he announced several times a week in tribal drinking and eating places on the urban reservation that he would argue and represent the expressed needs of tribal people. He answered the telephone call in his office.

"Tell me trouble with a smile," he said.

"I have to stop drinking. . . . My children are gone and this is my last dime, please don't hang up. . . . I have to stop drinking. I am cold, someone took my winter coat last night," she told. Even her voice shivered from the cold.

"Where are you?" asked the advocate.

"In a booth by the Band Box on Tenth Avenue near Chicago," she said.

"Who are you?"

"Marleen . . . Marleen American Horse Peterson."

The tribal advocate told her to wait in the telephone booth until he arrived. He drove to the intersection, doubtful that she would be calling with her last dime and with no winter clothes. But she was there and what she said was the truth. She huddled in the front seat of the car, shivering from the cold and trembling from her need for alcohol.

She sat in the kitchen of the Neighborhood House drinking black coffee, eating rolls, and retelling stories about her children, her birthplace and losses, and her last dime. The muscles on her face twitched when she spoke. Her lips were swollen. She was hesitant in her gestures, but she said she had to keep talking to keep from breaking down in tears.

"Nothing is left for me now."

"There never was anything, except, perhaps, a fantastic lover now and then," he said, shrugging his shoulders and smiling. He was sitting on his desk looking out the window while he sipped his coffee and waited for her response to his humor. His manner was affectionate and direct, but he spoke in a firm voice, harsh at times, showing humor and provoking arguments at the same time. He forced tribal people to speak in anger, to show their rage. An obligation, he once told his friends, to express fear and courage, the hard lessons he learned from his own poor childhood. He refused to accept dependencies in tribal people. He would sooner insult and provoke tribal people than to encourage dependencies. As a tribal advocate, he was loved and hated, but he was never mistrusted.

"But this drinking is killing me. . . ."

"Sometimes we are worth killing," he said.

"My children are gone," she pleaded.

"Change comes from within," he said, watching her face muscles as he spoke. "Through your dark eyes, and when you have dark skin the change is never simple. . . . White people think we are simple, simple like children and animals, pets, and we learn their simple words for our own problems and failures. . . . So now, this morning, before you stop drinking, you do want to stop drinking, right?"

"Yes, please help me do that."

"No one else will help you, but the first thing to do now is to unwind the tribe from the white words we have become. . . . Not forever, because white people are humorous and pleasant at times, but now we want to find out what those white words about your problem mean in your head. . . ."

"Can you commit me as an alcoholic?"

"No problem, but not for openers. . . . Listen now, drink your coffee and listen, white words have become part of the problem, white expectations, because we are held down, stuck in our own problems, through the language of white people. . . ."

"I have a terrible headache."

"Close your eyes while you listen and let your stomach go, relax your stomach, you are sitting too tense," he said, touching her shoulders. "Now just let your stomach go and let your legs go, take a short nap now while you listen for a few more minutes. . . . We are living in an impossible dream as winners and failures. . . . We are taught to be failures for the winners and then we must be grateful to those who are pledged to help us through the problems defined in white words. . . . We should all be at war with words, word wars, because we have been historical losers.

"We are treated like children in a new school on the first morning of classes, words are like prisons then, new controls, learning, the definitions of tribute to the teachers. And we are taught to praise those who detain and define us in simple words, disagreement is defined as being a loser, and when we speak our own language, not tribal languages now, but the languages of our hearts and our experiences, the tongue of our hearts, we are shunned or punished for speaking without manners.

"But you are not a child, you are not made out of white words, you are Marleen American Horse, a beautiful tribal drunk, a special sort of alcoholic from the reservation, a troubled visitor in the cities, wandering and warning the people about the coming doom, becoming the doom, you pass greetings from the urban reservation. . . . When you accept the worst words from drinking places in white minds you become dependent on the definitions, and dependent on the word cures. Are you a white person?"

"No, of course not, you can see that."

"Then how come you have a white problem?"

"What white problem?" she asked.

"Drunken Indian."

"But I want my three children back. . . . I keep trying to stop drinking, honest, this morning, honest. . . ."

"No money is all that stops you now," he said.

"Well, that's why I'm here, for someone to help me."

"The reason you are here makes no difference to me," he said, lighting a hand-rolled cigarette and offering it to her. He then rolled a second cigarette while he continued talking. "But listen, do you think people can help you to stop drinking?"

"Well, yes, someone can," she answered.

"Who will help? Name a person or place now."

"Some agencies."

"Which ones will help you?"

"The ones for drinking," she said.

"But those agencies speak white words about your problem. . . . The cause of the problem is not the cure in words unless you are a trickster or a warrior. . . . But you are a drunk, in white words you are an alcoholic, and a good one because you have have lost everything, and we all know that people from reservations have drinking problems in white languages. Can the words that define your problem become the cure for your problem, cures in the same words that created the problem?"

"What are you talking about?"

"Word wars."

"What does that mean?" she asked.

"Will words change you?"

"Well, no, not to change, not words. . . ."

"Then how come you have been sitting there, smoking a hand-rolled cigarette, drinking coffee and listening to me tell you that I love you, I love you too much to deceive you. . . . This is no cure in words, answers are not cures, words are not cures, ceremonies are cures, but not oaths and promises and the bullshit language of cures. . . . These are dependencies. Word cures are like eating

menus for dinner and wondering why our children still hunger. . . .
Word cures cause internal word wars. . . . Words have power when
words are not over the counter cures."

"But what can I do, no one cares."

"Care for yourself. . . . If you must drink, then drink in good
humor, drink with the courage of a warrior and feel good, but never
drink as a problem. Caring for yourself is not drinking like a white
word problem and feeling guilty about it later."

"I am afraid, and I need a drink."

"Then you must learn how to drink without guilt," he said in a
softer tone of voice. "But if you were free from guilt then you would
not need to drink for any reason. . . . What I am trying to say
like a trickster, the sad news, the bottom line, is that there are few
people who will help you."

"But you will."

"Here are the choices this morning," he said in a more business-
like tone of voice. "Look at it this way, there are three choices for
now: one, you can come home with me and I will take care of you
and then you can come to work with me and learn how to help
others with their drinking problem, so that you can cure yourself
by making other people feel guilty.

"Two, we can try to find an agency or hospital to receive you
for treatment as an alcoholic. You can take the cure if someone
will take you.

"Three, I can sign a complaint and have you committed to a so-
phisticated drunk tank for six months where they may or may not
help you. . . . Which is it this morning?"

"Commit me."

"No," he said.

"But I don't have any money or clothes, nothing."

"Money is not the problem," he said, opening a large book con-
taining a list of social service agencies in the state. "We can find the
money, but first let's call every agency in this book, every agency
in the city, and you listen in on the extension while I tell them
about you and what your problem is and then you will see who

will help you. . . . My guess is that every agency will first make an excuse that they can't help for some technical reason and then refer you to another agency. . . . Perpetual referral is a guiding principle in social services to the poor. The idea is to keep poor people, and people with problems, running from agency to agency on referral until they get mean or tired and stop asking. Agencies are made out of words and word cures and referrals are the best cures they know."

The tribal advocate called several agencies during the morning. Not one of them could help and all of them referred the client to another place. Marleen American Horse listened on the extension to the conversations. In the beginning she was embarrassed to hear people talking about her, but then she became depressed and discouraged. Late in the afternoon, when the advocate had called the last of the agencies, her depression disappeared in sudden bursts of laughter. She smiled and laughed through the last word referral cures over the telephone.

"This is where we started," said the advocate.

"But not like this morning when I called," she said.

"Which is it now?"

"Thank you for the offer, but I would not feel good going home with you. I would feel in the way and like trouble, you know, so I guess you should commit me. . . ."

"No, not unless you're drunk."

"No, no more drinking," she said.

The advocate, the tribal trickster and realist, took a business card with his name and two telephone numbers printed on it and taped two dimes to the front. "This," he said, handing the card to her, "is your commitment ticket. . . . When you get drunk again, call me at any time at either of these numbers and tell me where you are drinking and I will have you committed."

The advocate supplied her with clothing, a winter coat, a room with the rent paid for one month, cash to live for two weeks, which was drawn from a special fund to assist tribal people. Then he took her to dinner. The two of them talked about the weather, her birthplace before the flood, their children, their travels, old memories, dreams, fantasies, love and being loved, and then she asked him to leave her at the same telephone booth she used to call him in the morning.

She smiled when she left the car and waited near the telephone booth until he drove away. The advocate never heard from her again.

LAUREL HOLE IN THE DAY

aurel Hole In The Day opened her mouth to speak, her lips
moved to shape the first words, but she could not tell her
impossible dream. She stood in silence in the Waite Neighborhood House kitchen, dressed in a new colorful print dress. Tears
were dripping down her plump brown cheeks.

Laurel could hear her voice inside, but when the words took
shape on her lips her throat tightened and she could not speak. She
knew that if she forced but one word, a single word into sound, it
would burst with all the dreams and emotional pain and loneliness
from her heart like a bird at dusk against a window.

"Would you like coffee?" the advocate asked, knowing that
neighborhood houses were not the best places to break down and
then wait for the spirits to return.

Laurel nodded in a positive manner.

"Would you like to talk about something?"

Laurel nodded in a positive manner.

"Too serious to speak about?"

Laurel nodded in a positive manner.

"You must be pregnant," said the tribal advocate.

Laurel smiled and lowered her head. She was married with nine children; the youngest child was having surgery for a cleft pallet. The public health officers on the White Earth Reservation had made arrangements for Laurel Hole In The Day and her husband Peter to live in Minneapolis for one week while their infant daughter recovered. A small three-room tar-paper house, sitting up high on blocks, has been their home on the reservation since their marriage.

Laurel lived in Minneapolis when she was seventeen, at the end of the war, working as a laborer in a federal defense plant. When her future husband was discharged, she moved back to the reservation with him because he had seen too much during the war and wanted to live alone with his new wife in the woods.

Laurel was not pregnant. She loved children but she told her husband that nine was enough. She was too old now, she told him. He smiled then and thought about the times he made love with her deep in the woods where no one could hear them. No one but the birds and animals and trees to hear them. Laurel loved this lonesome man, but she remembered the time when she worked at the defense plant and talked with interesting people. Now, standing alone in a neighborhood house near the urban reservation without him, she could not tell that her impossible dream was to leave the violence of the reservation and live in an apartment in the city. She lifted her face to the tribal advocate and moved her lips again, but she could not make a sound. Silence had taken her dream from her memories and would not give it back that morning.

"Would you answer some questions?"

Laurel nodded in a positive manner.

"In ten questions, one through ten, you will tell me what you are not able to tell me," said the advocate. He lighted a hand-rolled cigarette and started his examination to reveal the secret cause of her silence.

"Are you down from the reservation?"

Laurel nodded in agreement. The tribal advocate escorted her to his office located near the front of the old mansion. There he instructed her to point to her reservation on a map. She pointed to Pine Point, a small village on the White Earth Reservation, and then tapped the map in that place.

"Do you live with your husband?"

Laurel nodded in a positive manner.

"How many children do you have?"

Laurel raised nine fingers.

"Do you need a place to live here?"

Laurel nodded in a positive manner.

"Is there someone in prison or in the hospital?"

Laurel nodded in agreement and then covered her face with her small hands. In a few minutes she held out her fingers and counted to nine on them, stopping and emphasizing the ninth finger, her ninth child.

"Do you have work?" the advocate asked.

Laurel nodded in a negative manner.

"Do you need money to live?"

Laurel nodded in a positive manner.

"When will you return to the reservation?"

Laurel held up five fingers.

"Five days and you want work and a place to live?"

Laurel nodded with enthusiasm.

"Impossible, an impossible dream," said the tribal advocate, walking back and forth in his small office. He opened the window and looked outside at the trees.

Laurel lowered her head.

"Is your husband a bear or a bird?"

Laurel looked up, moved her lips in the shape of doubt or suspicion and then smiled, covering her mouth with her small hands.

The tribal advocate placed two pieces of blank paper on the table in front of her and told her to list what she wanted on the first piece of paper, her impossible dream, and to list on the second piece of paper what she saw as the problems.

"Write about the bear and the dream first," he said and then left the room. When he returned a few minutes later she had completed her assignment.

The dream: We want to live with our children in the city together. We need a place to live and my husband wants to work so to pay the rent on time. This is all. Did your dad work for the tribal council once?

The problems: My youngest daughter is in the hospital ward getting better now. She is very sick and she will be able to talk when she grows up because of the operation. Peter is there with her, we do not have money and no work so we could not pay the rent right away. Peter has a bad back from the woods. I hope you can help us, we got to go back next week on Monday. The public health nurse takes care of us now, and the children at home.

Migwetch and thank you,

Laurel Hole In The Day

The tribal advocate told her to come back in three days with her husband. Meanwhile, he said, he would do what could be done to fulfill her impossible dream with a place to live, furnishings, work, money, and good humor. She smiled and he held her soft hands. Tears came to her eyes when he told her that he understood and admired her courage to dream, "and your courage to come here, to a stranger, to tell me your dream without being able to speak. . . .

"It was the trickster that made me ask you about being pregnant and if your husband was a bear or a bird, which is he? It was a moment of humor to keep me together here in your powerful silence.

"I have one last request," he said, looking out the window. "Show me, will you bring your husband with you and talk when you come back in three days?"

Laurel nodded in a positive manner.

"You are beautiful," he said.

She left the neighborhood house through the back door, the servants' entrance when the old mansion was owned by the elite and served by the poor, the same door where she had entered.

The impossible dream was impossible on the income from one unskilled worker, unless the couple separated and she applied for welfare assistance. The best working arrangement the tribal advocate could find on short notice was with a small firm where the husband and wife could work. The company manufactured and assembled caps for glue bottles. They could survive on that income until better work could be found. The employer agreed to pay them both by the week.

Next the advocate found a small three-bedroom apartment in an ancient fourplex on the urban reservation a few blocks from Franklin Avenue. The owner, a despicable overweight slumlord who smoked stout cigars, the reincarnation of the evil gambler from the tribal past, agreed to provide a six-month lease and two weeks' free rent on the condition that the tenants paint the whole apartment and fix the door at their own expense. The advocate arranged to charge the paint to the Waite Neighborhood House and asked the director to send their maintenance worker over to fix the doors and windows.

When Laurel and Peter Hole In The Day returned three days later the advocate made them an offer. Peter smiled, he had lived too long in the woods since the war, and Laurel turned her head back and praised the good spirits in a gentle voice.

"But on one condition," said the advocate. "You must agree, in writing, never to feel obligated or indebted to me or to this house. . . . What will make me feel better is to become part of your family.

"Now, you can move in and start work tomorrow, but first you should meet your new employer and then I will call the public health people, speaking as your official social worker—we have friends at the hospital who will share in our conspiracies—and tell them to extend their support for one additional week to care for your infant daughter, which will give you both enough time to get settled."

The Hole In The Days met their new employer and after a few moments of romantic hunting and fishing talk, when he learned the couple were from the reservation, he explained the glue-cap operation. His description was more than enough to drive even bad dreams back to the woods forever. That Peter Hole In The Day came from the woods made the lesson even more painful for the tribal advocate. But his was an impossible dream, and before realities could catch up with them on the glue-cap assembly line, the advocate would find them more interesting work with better salaries.

The man was thrilled to explain his operation, to tell his friends that he had two real tribal people from the reservation working on his line, and so he began at the beginning, with the machines. "You put the caps on the mandrils or moulding pins in sequence, going around twice, the blue caps on the red pins. . . . If the pin does not function or is not installed then push this reset index button which releases the escape mandrils. . . . Wait, and then when you see red pins coming around the corner you will know the pins are in. . . . The pins spiral up by vibration and ten drop through the slot at a time. Notice that if the seam separates from the mould line or a flashing it could catch in the feeder slot and pile up . . . watch and feel for the voids."

Their new employer spoke in the language of government manuals, and he exploited the poor with low salaries, but his profits were low and he was, for the most part, an honest person who cared for people, his gossip was humanistic, and he spoke well of his workers. He loves tribal people, because he loved to be in the woods hunting and fishing, and puts tribal people together with the woods in his impossible dream. The couple and their employer exchanged images in their impossible dream. He gave them an advance on their salaries.

The couple moved into their new apartment. The staff from the neighborhood house and other friends helped them paint the rooms. Their children came down from the reservation and in two months the advocate found them more suitable work, with insurance and other benefits, with larger companies.

Their impossible dream worked for several months, but while the couple was at work, other tribal people in the building and on the block, borrowed, which is called stealing in the white world, their food and made long-distance calls on their telephone.

Laurel said she wanted to move.

"But this is the urban reservation," said the advocate, pointing out that living in a white neighborhood could be even more uncomfortable.

"We work hard for nothing," she explained. "When we come home the door is broken down, even with our oldest children here, and people take everything. . . . We want to move away where we can be at peace."

"The reservation never changes. . . ."

The tribal advocate found them a comfortable house to rent in a white neighborhood on the northside. The rent was less than the cost of the apartment on the urban reservation. They saved their money, and with the increase in their salaries on the new job, they were able to buy a good used car.

But in six months the couple was living in loneliness, and together they turned at night to drinking with old friends in bars on the urban reservation. Peter was absent from work too often and was fired. Two weeks after that, when he picked up his last check, he disappeared with the car.

Laurel applied for welfare assistance and several months later, before summer, she moved with her children back to their tar-paper house on the White Earth Reservation. She found her husband back in the woods and gave up on her dream of living on the urban reservation.

BAPTISTE SAINT SIMON

Tribal fathers and sons seem to share a romantic reluctance to tell the truth in stories on each other. Baptiste Saint Simon, The Third, in a proud line of fur trading metis mixedbloods, was like that, praising his son, The Fourth. But when he turned sixteen the old metis leaned back on his backless reservation chair and told his son that he was stupid and a backward fool, and that even his best-shaped stories dropped from his thick mouth like chicken shit from the bottom of wet cardboard boxes.

Determined not to be a complete loser, Baptiste The Fourth, or Bat Four, as his few friends knew him on the reservation, took on the worst remarks from his father and fashioned his new manner on the tribal trickster model, hoping to balance the energies of good and evil in the world. But hard as he tried, and in good humor, he failed as a trickster and settled for the role of a fool. Evil was too much for him to balance. As a fool, a role that seemed to be his final mental and spiritual resting place, he was a brilliant success.

Bat Four never lost his need to depend on the scorn of his father and his father never said a good word about his son. One summer,

following a reservation solstice powwow, on the sl
Superior, Bat Four asked his father to validate his best
as a fool. His father leaned back on his backless resei
and told his son that he was a failure.

"When you are a fool, how can you be a success acting like a
fool, you are what you are, a fool," said Baptiste Saint Simon, The
Third.

Neither father nor son understood thoughts about form and content or culture and consciousness. Bat Four, performing from his
favorite being, acting out his own credulous career as a fool without
praise from his father, was his own form and content. He became
what he was in the beginning. He was his own act. To his credit, as
a fool in form and content, he became an expression of pure tribal
foolishness. Children who were not fools but admired his foolishness pretended to be fools in his image. He was not forgotten on
the reservation.

Bat Four was arrested by tribal police for stealing wine and underclothing from three white women campers. When he came before
the judge in tribal court, he explained that wine was medicine, sacred
medicine for his social medicine bundle. "No metis would steal
medicine because stolen medicine never works right," he explained.

"But there are witnesses who maintain that and then at the time
of the stealing you stole their wine and . . . whatever, do you now
maintain that you did or did not do this?" asked the judge in the
confused language he thought was legal. He smiled over the bench
at the white women campers.

"Me pleads the fifth commandment," said Bat Four.

"The what?" asked the judge.

"The fifth commandment," he repeated. His father, he knew,
would be proud of him because he told once about white people
covering their lies with the fifth commandment. "Medicine is not
a business, medicine is a secret, so, even if I did steal this medicine,
you know I never did it because people steal things, because people
who steal things always come back to the scene of the crime and I
never went back to the campgrounds, which proves it. . . ."

"What was that?" asked the judge.

"People who start fires do that," said Bat Four.

"Do what?"

"Go back to the scene of the fire," said Bat Four.

"But this is no fire."

"Not all fires are burning either."

The tribal judge pushed his short fingers through his black hair and frowned. The white women, seeing more humor than crime, withdrew their complaint and returned to the tribal campground on the lake. Nothing more was said about the wine or the underclothing. The judge dismissed the charges and then told Bat Four that "listening to you is like slipping backward and maintaining a vacuum of unspoken categories."

"You can count on me," said Bat Four.

When his father died and was buried, Bat Four spit four times in four directions on his grave and, giving up four generations of backless chairs and reservation fur trades, packed his bag and walked backward from the reservation. Children followed the fool down to the highway to the bus stop, walking backward. When the bus stopped he turned toward the children, his friends, nodded once, and said: "Never listen to your father, because if you do then his voice will get into your head and hold back all the words you want to speak." The door closed and the fool was gone.

Bat Four disappeared for a decade, but rumors traveled back to the reservation somehow, down the moccasin telegram, that he had married a white southern woman. She was a waitress at a truck stop, and she had been waiting too long for the perfect man to eat in her station. Happie Mansion was her birth name, and she pushed her tribal man to improve himself even more than her projected perfections. He completed a Dale Carnegie public-speaking course and learned a few social dances, but his rate of improvement was much slower than his southern woman had expected. On the summer night she heard his reservation stories for the fourth time she bought him a bus ticket going back north and turned back her clocks on perfection.

Bat Four arrived in Minneapolis in the morning, and before noon he was at work telling stories to the blonde social service volunteer at the church-supported center. She peeled an orange while she pretended to listen. Oranges settled her nerves.

"Let me never answer to the exaggerated claim that the rights of reasonable men, and women of course, who maintain their common confrontations in administrative situations," said Bat Four, smiling and changing the tone and moan of his voice from time to time according to the principles he learned in public-speaking courses.

"Real situations, centerfold cultures, sound agreements and pleasant preparations, must be part of the policies expressed by our leaders both here and on the reservations. . . . Corruptions are no less common than commodities on the reservation now. . . . No one should ever take a back seat to discrimination. . . . We need ideas to move us on, ideas like these, listen now, propinquity, peace, pride, for all the tribes be their color white or not and their tongues thick or forked. . . ."

"Do you need work?" asked the blonde.

"You said the overworked word," he responded.

"What can you do, what experience do you have?"

"I can do what you are doing."

"Well, this is not something you can do walking in from the streets." She defended her knowledge, even as a volunteer, of social services and her personal contacts in the world of work. "What I am doing here takes more than the desire to offer social services. . . . I know the employers and who to send them."

"Here I am for the sending," said Bat Four.

Her face tightened and her blue eyes narrowed.

Bat Four smiled and winked at her, first with the right eye and then with the left eye, and then with both. Her face hardened. She appeared indifferent but he could see hatred in her hands. She handed him a pencil and a blank form and told him to answer all the questions. "Then return it to me when you have finished. . . . You will find a table in the next room to work on." She used the complicated form to discourage people she did not think were suitable

for employment. Few people returned to her office with the completed application. But the fool was one who returned.

"Here we are, all done," said Bat Four.

She read over his entries on the application.

"Why do you say you are an Indian?" she asked, looking up at
him and examining his face. "You certainly don't look like one."

"What does one look like?" he asked.

"Well, not like you," she said beneath her breath.

"I notice you did not answer the question on the application
about being arrested. Have you ever been arrested? We must have
honest answers on the applications."

"Not too often, so I didn't fill it in."

"You have no real work record Mister Saint Simon, nothing too
much to go on here. Why did you leave your last place of employment?" she asked, shifting her bracelets up and down her forearm.

"No layoffs, so I quit."

"Where was that?"

"Way down south where the cotton grows."

"Do you have a drinking problem?" she asked, still looking for
problems. She shifted her feet under the desk and tapped her heels
on the wooden floor. She looked out the window when he answered
her questions.

Nothing would discourage him from *looking* for work. He was
pleased to sit and talk about work, even look for work from place
to place, but he never wanted to find work. Even the thought of
working within white time on the line upset his bowels. His last
job lasted three hours.

"Drinking is an art not a problem," responded Bat Four. "Some
people are better artists than others. . . . Take me for example, if
drinking was an inherited trait, you know, genetic predispositions
to holding stemmed glasses and wine bottles, I would be only half
as good as my darker brothers from the reservation. . . . But as
an art, well, there is no end to the possible forms and expressions
of drinking."

"Please answer the problem . . . the question."

"Some critics like my work with the bottle."

"You must answer the question," she insisted.

"There is some room for improvement in my drinking art," said Bat Four, winking at her again. Then he stood up and moved toward the window where he could stand in the center of her vision. "Here now, not all celebrations are created for museums."

"What is your address?" she asked.

"None for now, or is it not applicable?"

"You must have an address to find employment," she said, raising and lowering her arm so her bracelets slid up and down. Her voice was tense. She tried to discourage him from looking for work, but she had not been successful. "Without an address no one will hire you."

"This will be my address then."

"Here? No, this is not a place to live," she said.

"Well, it should be, let me be the first."

"Do you have a bag?" she asked.

"She returned to the truck stop," said Bat Four.

"No, I mean luggage," she said.

"I have my head through my suitcase."

"Impossible," she said under her breath.

"How good must I be to look for work?"

"Do you have an automobile?" she asked.

"I did once," responded Bat Four.

"What do you mean, once?"

"My father-in-law used it to go to the store."

"Then you have a car?"

"No, that was three years ago, he never returned from the store," said Bat Four, smiling and winking at the blonde. He was standing near the window.

"Do you have any money?"

"None."

"What do you do with your money?"

"Buy wine and then spend the rest foolishly."

"Do you have bad credit?" she asked.

"How do you think I got so far into debt?"

She noted on his application form that he could not be placed with a responsible firm. "Transient labor for this fool," she wrote. "Uncooperative and uncommunicative. All talk and no work." Then she looked up and smiled at him. Her stomach was upset from listening to him, and she needed to eat another orange to settle down. He smiled back and waited in silence. She handed him a referral card for the labor pool downtown.

"What is this place?" asked Bat Four.

"Labor pool," she said.

"Too much experience required there."

"Enough, enough, now I have other things to do."

"You have boiled eyes," said Bat Four.

"What?"

"Boiled eyes, the eyes of boiled fish."

"Get out, get out of here now," she snapped. She wagged the fingers on one hand toward the door and reached for the telephone with the other hand to call the director. "People like you make this a rotten place to work. . . . You give a bad name to your people, now get out of here before I call the police and have you removed."

"Not until you give me some money," he said.

"Money, the hell with you."

"Then call the police," said Bat Four. "How would that look here, here sits the blonde in her diamonds and she calls the police to get rid of a down-and-out mixedblood bow and arrow who did nothing more than tell her her eyes look like boiled fish . . . and they do. Social workers with boiled eyes. Give me enough to live and eat for a day, at least."

"Over my dead body," she said.

"I'll tell the director you're a racist."

"Stop this. . . ."

"What do you care, is it your money?" asked Bat Four.

She filled out a voucher for cash and then threw it on the floor. "Now get the hell out of here, take your cash and get the hell out of here and don't come back."

"Blondes with boiled eyes make poor volunteers."

Bat Four picked up the voucher, read it over, suggested a change in the amount of the cash payment, which she changed, and then slipped it into his shirt pocket. He winked at the blonde and then disappeared out the door.

Bat Four had enough cash to travel back to the reservation where he lived for the summer drinking wine and telling stories. He was the last mixedblood link in four generations of fur traders. Bat Four practiced his fur trade in words. His greatest misfortune was telling his best stories to mindless white women.

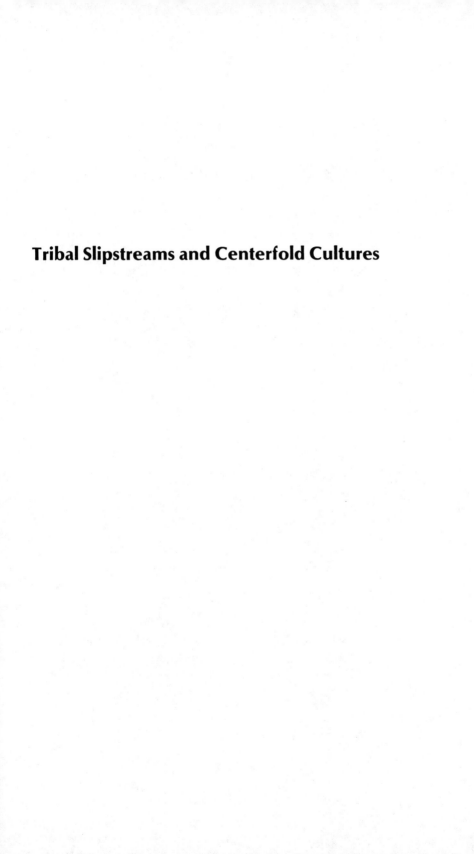

Tribal Slipstreams and Centerfold Cultures

CUSTER ON THE SLIPSTREAM

G eneral George Armstrong Custer, retouching the message that old generals never die, must hold the national record for resurrections. White people are stuck with his name, and his specter, in Custer, South Dakota and other places, but since the battle of the Little Bighorn the loathsome voice and evil manner of this devious loser prevail on hundreds of reservations. He is resurrected in humor and on white faces in the darkness.

The Chippewa, known as the Anishinabe in the language of the people, described the first white men as kitchi mokaman, which in translation means, the men with swords or "great knives." Since then the word has been shortened to chamokaman or chamok and the description has become depreciative and sardonic.

Farlie Border was a chamokaman and the resurrection of General George Custer. He lived for personal aggrandizement and worked for the United States Department of Labor. He was a proud and evil white man who exploited minorities and the poor for personal power and income. His manner, behind his needs for power, was devious. He laughed with unctuous humor. Federal agencies often found the most corrupt and incompetent administrators and paid them the highest salaries to work with the poor and disadvantaged. Custer and Border sought power and wealth in small places, and worked better under attack.

Farlie Border was resurrected as George Custer under the sign of Taurus, the second sign of the zodiac, but he was too stubborn to admit his celestial bearing. His personal gain games required the best tribal minds, sober and articulate, to survive and share the federal spoils. More ominous than the racial contests he staged in finding and placing tribal people in new paraprofessional careers was his appearance in the modern world. His white hair and brackish blue eyes, his gait and manner, the placement of his blunt white fingers when he spoke, the smile and the evil curl on his thick lips, were all from the tribal memories of General George Custer. The evil loser had been resurrected in a federal program to serve tribal people and the poor.

Tribal people who visited his office for the first time said later that they could smell leather and blood and horses on the prairie. Someone in his department called him general, mister general, at a public meeting for the poor. Border smiled and stacked his fingers one over the others on the table like bodies.

"Crazy Horse is here," his tall blonde secretary told him one morning. "He said he has an appointment with you from the past, but there is nothing on the calendar about him. . . . He looks too mean to think about before lunch."

"What ever turns him on. . . . First place a call to Clement Beaulieu and then send in the mean one when I am through talking to Beaulieu," said Border.

General Border passed most of his federal administrative time in a padded high-back office chair. He pitched backward in his chair and bounced the tips of his fingers together when he listened. The drapes were drawn closed. The floor was covered with an expensive thick bone-white carpet. A picture of a black panther, the animal, was mounted on one wall. Two posters were taped on the other wall opposite the window. One encouraged tribal people, through ecclesiastical shame, not to drop out of high school. The second poster pictured one sad tribal child, suffering from hunger and various diseases, walking without shoes on the hard earth. The printed message, "walk a mile in his moccasins," had been crossed out and changed to read, "don't walk in my moccasins now, I think I stepped in something." His sinister smile seemed to spread over the entire room.

"Beaulieu. . . . You mixedblood bastard."

"Nothing is certain," responded Beaulieu.

"Lunch?" asked Border.

"No."

"Selfish bastard. . . . Then at least tell me what Alinsky said last night. What are the new rules for radicals?" asked Border, pitching back in his high-back chair and closing his eyes to listen. He preferred telephone conversations with people because visual contacts made him nervous.

It was spring and the winter dreams of radicals and racial ideologies were budding into abstract forms. Saul Alinsky, the radical organizer and street-tough theoretician, was on his "zookeeper mentality" tour and had spoken at the Lutheran Redeemer Church in Minneapolis to a collection of fair-minded liberals. He said it was the issue and the action, not the skin color that made the difference in organizing for social changes.

"Alinsky blessed himself with cigarette smoke," said Beaulieu. "He smokes too much. He toured through the usual zookeeper shit . . . his social worker shockers and then defined power as amoral, power as having the ability to act. The liberals loved him. You should have been there. . . . Why do you fight being the great white liberal you are?"

"Be serious Beaulieu," said Border.

"Yes, this is a revolution, right?" said the mixedblood tribal organizer. "I remember two great lines from his speech: the tongue has a way of trapping the mind, and we are tranquilized by our own vocabulary. . . . He *is* one of the word warriors."

"More?"

"Never expect people to move without self-interest. . . . The white liberals there had no trouble knowing what that meant. Neither do you there Farlie Custer."

Silence.

"He also said color made the difference. . . ."

"The difference in what?"

"The difference in issues and actions."

"Bullshit! No white man said that," said Border.

"Listen to this," explained Beaulieu. "I was putting you on, color makes no difference for the moment, but the best part of the evening was a spontaneous speech made by an old bow and arrow, as George Mitchell says, one of the arrowstocracy. He called himself Sitting Bull one time and Crazy Horse the second time, one of the prairie arrowstocracy, and he moved forward through the old church with a loud voice, interrupting Alinsky. Saul took another cigarette and listened. No one had the courage to tell him to stop. He spoke your name."

Beaulieu remembered how silent the church was when the old arrowstocrat spoke:

"My people call me Sitting Bull. Listen here, who told you white skins to sit there feeling smug and stingy as tics on a mongrel when you should be out there, in the streets with the rats and cockroaches, all over this land, burning down the Bureau of Indian Affairs?

"The Bureau is yours, your government made it up, and it is killing us while you sit in here talking and talking like ducks on a crowded pond. The white man has been killing us since he first drifted off course and got lost on the shores of our great mother earth. . . .

"Now our pockets are empty and mother earth is polluted and stripped for coal and iron. Why are you all sitting here listening to talking about talking from a white man? My name is Crazy Horse, remember that, you'll hear it again. My people are the proud Sioux. Listen, there are things to tell now. The white man puts himself in our way everywhere. Look at that Border and the Bureau, Custer is sitting everywhere holding up the Indians. Now all the original people on our mother earth go through white men and stand in lines for everything. The white man tries to make us like you to sit and listen to white people talking about talking about money and things and good places to live away from the poor.

"What would the white man do if he didn't have our problems to talk about? Think about all the people who are paid to talk about us and our so-called problems. Who would social workers be without us? Tell me this. Who would they be? They'd be out of work, that's where they'd be now. . . .

"But they are wrong, all wrong. The land will be ours again. Watch and see the land come back to us again. The earth will revolt and everything will be covered over with new earth and all the whites will disappear, but we will be with the animals again, we will be waiting in the trees and up on the sacred mountains. We will never assimilate in places like this. This church . . .

"There just ain't enough jobs in the Bureau of Indian Affairs to keep us all quiet. Everywhere else the government restores the nations they defeat in wars. Do you know why the Indian nations, the proudest people in the whole world, were never restored? Do you know why? You, all you white faces, do you know? The answer is simple, see how dumb white people are. This is the answer, listen now, because we were never defeated, never defeated, that is the answer. . . .

"Everywhere else in the world the white government sends food and medicine to people who are hungry and sick but not to the Indians. We get nothing, nothing, because the white man never defeated us, but he makes his living on us being poor. The white man needs us to be poor for his sick soul. We got nothing because we have never been defeated, remember that. . . .

"The white government puts people everywhere in our way, trying to defeat us with words now and meetings so we can be helped. But we still dance, see. The road to evil and hell will never be laid with feathers from our sacred eagles. We are the people of the wind and water and mountains and we will not be talked into defeat, because we know the secrets of mother earth, we talk in the tongues of the sacred earth and animals. We are still dancing. When we stop dancing then you can restore us. . . .

"Remember me. Remember me talking here. My face is here before you. My name is Crazy Horse and when I talk the earth talks through me in a vision. I am Crazy Horse. . . ."

When he stopped talking he lowered his head, fitted his straw hat on his head over his braids, drew his scarred finger under his nose, and then walked in a slow shuffle down the center of the church and through the center doors to the outside.

Alinsky lighted another cigarette.

"Catch you later Custer," said Beaulieu.

"Fuck you Beaulieu," said Farlie Border, dropping the telephone and stroking his white beard. He sat back and remembered the first time he encountered a tribal person. The experience still haunts him at night. It was in northern Wisconsin where his parents had a summer cabin. Border had seen people with dark skin from a distance, his parents called them savages, but it was not until he was fifteen that he had his first real personal encounter.

He was watching the sun setting behind the red pines across the lake when he heard several dogs barking. Young Border opened the door of the cabin and no sooner had he focused on four reservation mongrels chasing a domestic black cat than the animals turned around twice and ran past him into the cabin. The four mongrels knocked him down in the door. He stood up again, the cat reversed the course and he was knocked down a second time when the dogs came out of the cabin. Then, in a rage, he took his rifle, which was mounted near the back door, and shot at the cat and two mongrels before an old tribal man grabbed his arm and knocked him to the ground. Border rolled over and sprang back on his feet ready to fight, but reconsidered when he came face to face with four tribal people. The faces smiled at him and pointed at his white hair. At first the tribal people teased him, speaking part of the time in a tribal language. They called him an old woman with white hair, but then, recognizing a historical resurrection, he was named General George Custer.

"Custer, you killed our animals."

"Wild animals," said Border to the four faces.

"Everything is wild, little Custer."

"But the mongrels attacked me," pleaded Border.

"Now you must pay for our animals."

"You must pay us for the wild," said another face.

"How much?" asked Border.

"Ten thousand dollars," said a third dark face.

"How much?"

"Ten million dollars," said a fourth dark face.

"What did you say?" Border asked again.

"Then return the land to wild," said the old man.

"What wild?"

"Your cabin and the land is ours."

Border resisted their demanding voices and became arrogant and hostile. He demanded that his rifle be returned and made a detracting remark about tribal people. The tribal faces smiled and mocked his words and manners, and then touched him again and pulled at his white hair. Border was furious and lunged at the old man, but the old tribal shaman stepped aside like a trickster. Border tripped and fell to the ground.

"This is wild land," said the old man. "This has been tribal land since the beginning of the world. . . . What you know is nothing. Custer has taken your heart."

Border spit on the old man.

"Custer has returned," said the old man.

"Rotten savages," said Border.

The sun had set behind the red pines.

Silence.

The old man motioned with his hands and then hummed ho ho ha ha ha haaaa. . . . Border was weakened under the gaze of the old man. Then he was overcome with dizziness. Moments later, he

has never been sure how much time passed, he regained consciousness. His rifle was gone. His eyes were crossed and his vision was
weakened. He could not see straight for several hours. Border still
dreams about falling with the setting sun into deep black pools, like
the deep dark eyes of the old tribal man who possessed him with
his shamanic powers.

Border bounced his fingers together.

The office was too warm.

"My name is Crazy Horse," he said, standing inside the office
door on the bone-white carpet. "Sitting Bull and Crazy Horse and
I have come down here to see you alone. . . . I came on the rails
not on relocation. Need some cash now, not much, but enough to
make it for a time. . . . And some work, hard to find work, like
your work, whatever you can find me to do well."

Border turned in his high-back chair. Looking toward the floor,
avoiding eye contact, he saw that Crazy Horse was wearing scuffed
cowboy boots and tight blue jeans. His crotch was stained and his
shirt was threadbare at the elbows. He rolled his own cigarettes and
carried a leather pouch of loose tobacco lashed to his belt.

"Crazy Horse is the name. . . ."

Border said nothing. While he watched his hands he thought about
the old tribal man at the cabin. Crazy Horse cracked his knuckles
and then hooked his thumbs under his belt. Tattoos, wearing thin
on his fingers, spelled "love" on the left and "hate" on the right
hand.

Crazy Horse waited on the white carpet. The longer he waited for
recognition the more he smiled. He bumped the brim of his western
straw hat with his thumb, tipping it back from his forehead. His
right ear moved with ease when he smiled. Animals knew more about
smiling than people, animals knew that when he smiled and moved
his ear in a certain way, it meant that he was in spiritual control of
the situation. He survived much better when white people did not
speak, because words, too many words, loosened his concentration
and visual power.

Silence.

Border was breathing faster. The veins in his neck throbbed harder and his stomach rose in sudden shifts beneath his light-blue summer suit. Border turned and looked into the face of the stranger. His eyes were deep black pools. Border could not shift his focus from Crazy Horse. He was being drawn into the dark pools, the unknown, he was falling in his vision. His arms tingled and his head buzzed, but before he slipped from consciousness into the deep dark pools of tribal shamanism, he sprang from his chair with the last of his energy, like a cat, leaped across the white carpet and struck at the tribal face with his white fists again and again until he lost his vision and consciousness. He was peaceful then. Face down on the deep white carpet he could smell the prairie earth that dropped from the boots of the shaman.

"Border, wake up . . . wake up, wake up."

Silence.

Border came back to his time in consciousness, but he was uncertain, he wondered if he could travel forever from the place he had been on the floor. His vision was weak, colors were less distinct, sunlight was blurred as it fell through the windows in the outer offices, blurred as it was when the old tribal man hexed him at the cabin. He did recognize the shapes of familiar faces around him, his fellow federal employees. The women rubbed his arms and face, and then the men lifted him into his high-back chair.

Silence.

"Where is that man?" asked Border.

"What man?"

"That man called Crazy Horse."

"Crazy Horse?"

"Crazy Horse, peculiar name of course," his secretary explained. "Well, he waited for a few minutes, not too long, and then left while you were on the telephone . . . but he did say he would be back sometime."

Farlie Border shivered in his sleep for months. His dreams were about people falling into deep pools, dark pools, people he could not reach. In some dreams he saw his own face in the pools, slipping under before he could reach himself. To balance his fear and boredom with his work he turned to visual and mechanical thrills. He ingested hallucinogenic drugs, subsidized bizarre sexual acts, bought a police radio so he could be at the scene of accidents, and drove a powerful motorcycle.

Border disappeared late in the summer. White people said he was teaching at a college for women, but tribal rumors held that his vision crossed coming around a curve at high speed on his motorcycle and he died in the wind space behind a grain truck . . . slipping from grace in a slipstream.

FRUIT JUICE
AND TRIBAL TRICKERIES

irlie Blahswomann, South Dakota born mixedblood prom queen turned Kundalini yogi, murmurs "ho hum here now ho ho ho ho one more morning at the freeword ports," and then tows her wide half-white thighs through the narrow wicket into her fruit wagon.

To the bubblemakers in plastic clothes, thin and trim campus butterflies, and the street culture evangels, Girlie is known as the Sather Gate Juicer at the University of California in Berkeley. She squeezes fruits and tribal fantasies to the last drop, smiles and touches her nose and ears too much, but she knows now she would rather make juice than social work the poor on the reservation again.

Six mornings a week, during the past ten months, her lover, Slowarrow, the patois name a logger gave him because he moves too slowly in the woods, huffs and puffs and pushes her fruit wagon three blocks down Telegraph Avenue to Bancroft Way from the overnight parking lot to the campus entrance. Fruit wagon in proper place, wicket closed, Slowarrow keeps his mixedblood woman Girlie supplied with oranges and grapefruits until dark.

"Here now ho ho ho. Two more months from now," the mixed-blood juicer soughs over and over slipping her blunt fingers into blue rubber mitts and slicing three rows of ripe oranges on the rough wooden block near the hand-powered juicer.

"Here now ho hum three more months."

"Ho who said that?" asks Girlie.

"Ho hum four more months."

"Where are you?" she asks, looking in the corners.

"Ho hum five more months."

"Who are you?"

"Ho hum six . . . seven . . . eight more months."

Girlie moans "never never never now" as she twirls the juicer handle down down down on the orange halves. "That super protein power is going to my head, giving me some kind of talking hallucinations," she said, looking up to the colorprint map tacked to the ceiling of her fruit wagon. Visual memories, reservations, places from the tribal past, places she has lived, are organized outside her mind on maps. She moves her thoughts over medium territories from the prairie to the desert and speaks to her friends and Kundalini families through printed place-names on the map. Her focus shifts and settles with her communal tribal cousins living at the Cheyenne River Reservation in South Dakota.

"Ho hum nine more months," the voice continues.

"Medium orange," a voice orders.

"Never never never now," she wails while she shifts her focus from the White Earth Reservation in Minnesota, where she once had a fine lover, to the place she wandered in the Sangre de Cristo mountains in New Mexico. "No more than two more here now. . . ."

"Did you hear that voice?" she asks a customer.

"Ho hum over here now," said the voice.

"Where, where?" pleaded Girlie.

"Over here ho ho ho ho," said the compassionate tribal trickster Erdupps MacChurbbs, one of the little people from the woodland reservations, snapping through fruit wagon time and space from the stack of orange boxes to the cash drawer and then from the map to the plastic service window.

Girlie first saw the woodland sprite sitting on the rim of the speaking hole. She smiled back at the tribal trickster, relieved that the voice she heard came not from protein farina hallucinations but from a real person, however small. "Good friends will know me now ho ho ho ho," she said, wiping her tears with blue rubber fingers which spread orange pulp on her cheeks.

Girlie was born poor on the reservation and then, with a federal scholarship, studied social work in college. When she returned to the reservation to help her people, taking up the romantic notions of social service fostered in the dominant culture, she was shunned as a white person would have been. With her dreams disintegrating, dreams she shared with white people, she became silent and depressed. She was losing her humor and good cheer, so, on a clear winter morning she packed her car and drove to San Francisco determined never to return to the reservation. In the watercities she found new friends among the mixedbloods there while she learned to live with her changing identities. The food she eats is an example. Now she eats Kundalini protein to be a good little yogi, but once or twice a week she drives to a remote shopping center where she removes her white turban, unfurls her dark tribal hair, and downs fastfood hamburgers in remembrance of her time past on the reservation.

"Tell me where you are now little one. . . . The great yogi from somewhere told me once that little voices would come to mind from undisciplined places, random worlds and lust words, and when that happened he said two weeks on boiled beets would cure the voices and the complexion." Girlie lowered her head from the ceiling map to the speaking hole.

"We are the words we speak tribal Girlie."

"Where are you now?"

"Up here now ho hum," said MacChurbbs, snapping though space from the speaking hole back to the ceiling map. He rests on his elbows, chin in hands, over the watercities beneath the hills.

"How can you do that there now?" asks Girlie.

"These names are not the territories little Girlie," said the tribal trickster through the stubborn and pedantic voice of the semanticist Alfred Korzybski.

"Upsidedown there?"

"Insideout down there now?" said the trickster.

"Who are you?" she asked.

"Call me little Deth . . . Deth," said MacChurbbs.

"Oh no not death now."

"Deth the deathless trickster. . . . Not the death of your terminal creeds and superfeeds. . . . Medium Deth from doubleback worlds in the language of out loud old doublespeak Seth," said the tribal trickster.

"Seth from Seth speaks fame?"

"Seth is dead but this is his new voice Deth speaking from halfcocked places and tilted dreams. . . . This is tribal trickster Deth on the unlevel speaking as the woman in me through the little medium of the tribal man in you little mixedblood Girlie. . . ."

"Ho ho ho no sir not the man in me here now. . . . Down with that father person, that reservation patriarch, and his name in me again."

"Listen to Deth speaking through you now:

"He named me Girlie Blahsmann and how I did love to twirl my new baton with all the other girls and dance in my feathers and white boots at the tribal parades and powwows and federal school football games until that evil white coach did things to our beavers in the locker room. . . . Father, who worked in land management for the Bureau of Indian Affairs, made fun of me because I was a woman. 'Girlie,' he said, 'Girlie, Girlie, you will be forever my little Girlie,' but when the radical tribal feminists at college shamed me into changing my name, father took back his love. Mother was a fullblood, she thought too much, it showed in her eyes, but she said little. . . . She married a white man to give her children a chance to live in a world without being poor. Some chance, I have given up on her sacrifices. The living is so much better here than on the reservation. . . . Father wanted me to change my name back to blah blah man and act like a proper woman, which means shaving my legs and pits and wearing dresses, for him, or getting married to a good provider with short hair. The way I am now he never wants me to come back to the reservation, sometimes he thinks he is more Indian than Indians are. . . .

"Ho hum ho ho ho that was five years ago now and the feminists ran me ragged with dumbshit duties worse than shaving and doing the dishes for a man, so I took to these maps you see and the personal awareness of inner spheres to keep me together. . . ."

"Shame on turning the outer spheres into inner spheres," said MacChurbbs as he hopscotched south over the watercities, Albany, Berkeley, Oakland, and back again on the ceiling map.

"Inner spheres now. Listen here, I attended the Institute for Postural Integration, Fort Help, and Le Center du Silence. . . . Studied at the Holistic Life University, audited programs at Dare to Dream, the Center for Conscious Human Living, which was more like thinking about thinking about living than living, and then there was the Laughing Man Institute, the feminists fought me about that . . . Dancing Fool and Ishmael House, and then settled for Kundalini yoga at the end because at least the brothers and sisters are clean and they had a comfortable place to live together. . . . But I will never forget my tribal past here, never. . . ."

"Girlie Kundalini insideout spheres," said MacChurbbs.

"Here now, in five years I have studied pastlives counseling, folk dancing, spontaneous exchange, the martial arts, all of them, consumer action, aura cleaning, hoof and mouth message, reincarnation communcation, and scenario sympathies.

"What spheres are you down now?"

"Here now in two months, two more months, no more here," she said twirling the juicer handle down on the oranges. "I want to travel and visit the Dharma King his Holiness Gyalwa Karmapa who is the spiritual head of the Kagyu order of Tibetan Buddhism. . . . He likes tribal people."

"What then little Girlie?" asked MacChurbbs.

"Then, well then I want to follow the humpback whales and listen and learn their ancient songs," she said as she punched a button on a small tape recorder with her blue rubber covered finger. The fruit wagon filled with the wailing and screeching voices of whales.

"And then there is nothing more to do, so I could return to the reservation and find an old shaman to live with, shave my legs if he cares and have some children, good place to raise them in the hills, and maybe work part-time in an abusement park. . . . Did you get that pun, abusement park?"

"Harmless abusement," said MacChurbbs.

"Tell me now is death still speaking in me here? Where have you been traveling little death? Where are you from now?" she asked.

"With Cisneros and Baldwin for the past few months," said MacChurbbs snapping back to the speaking hole, "we have been traveling through the deserts in search of seeing and the tribal secrets of translation . . . total translation."

"More little death, talk more, while I fix these people their orange drinks. . . . I can hear while I work," she said squeezing twelve oranges in a row.

"Archbishop Jiminez de Cisneros, the one who will lead us to simpler lives and high moral standards, and Monica Baldwin, who lived in total silence and seclusion in a convent for twenty-eight years, much before your overexamined inner and outer spheres of living. . . . Baldwin had a distant uncle who was Prime Minister of England, but that is a different time to tell. . . . We have visited various missions, spiritual communes, and tribal rancherias on the faults of the earth near the sea. . . . Some souls seek the secret faults of fools."

"Monica Baldwin," asked Girlie as she twirled the juicer handle down down down on the oranges, "is she a little person?"

"We are not little," said MacChurbbs as he snapped from the speaking hole to her nose. "Now look me in the eye and say that. We are the same when we learn to see ourselves alone. . . . People are not commodities to be compared by size and price. In all the places you have studied has no one taught you how to see and move through tribal time and space? Have all your worlds become word wars?" MacChurbbs kicked chunks of orange pulp from her cheeks.

"Two tribal clowns told me to compare things. . . . Tell me now little trickster, are little men lesser fools?" she asked, wrinkling her nose.

"Clowns raise humor like bread," said Monica Baldwin from the speaking hole. She was sitting next to MacChurbbs and wearing a dark suit with a vest. When she smiled she snapped from view.

"Words settle on dumb animals like terminal creeds. . . . Your vision is rerecorded in your head unsided and backward," said Mac-Churbbs. "You have turned tribal secrets into white words."

"Fools on the faults near the sea dress themselves each morning like clowns for abusement and new histories," said the archbishop. He was dressed in a dark green dalmatic. "The past has them waiting down near the edge planning their surprises."

"Not so hard little ones," pleaded Girlie.

"You are so small after all, so much commonsense to remember now, changing names, running your breath in numbers to some religious order, owning your dreams," said Baldwin as she skipped with MacChurbbs across the sacred mesas on the map in New Mexico.

"Well, now," said Girlie, wiping her nose with blue rubber fingers, "what can we ever do with me. . . . The prom was beautiful and father blah blah manages reservation land for white ranchers. . . . What can we do with me?"

"Ideologies and identities have a sudden opening and closing in tribal fruit wagons all over the world," said the archbishop. "Nothing but silence can be translated."

Silence.

The three little sprites snapped through the speaking hole in the service window and then rode all morning through common campus time and space on the backs of academic animals.

FEEDING

THE RESERVATION MONGRELS

ribal reservations are never the same from place to place, nor are the people who live on federal enclaves, but if some reservations went to the dogs, testing a trite idea with uncertain experiences, life would go on more or less as usual. Some tribal mongrels would be vindictive and punitive toward some humans, remembering the cold winters with too little to eat, but for the most part the mongrels on reservations would bark, as humans have spoken, at the usual number of pedigreed white poodles, canine police officers, terrier anthropologists, spaniel school teachers, and tell fine stories in the best oral tribal traditions.

Lilith Mae Farrier, a fine example of a trite living idea, loves animals with a blind devotion. She views living and breathing as a concept for living like animals. The mongrels loved her, all of them, but under tribal humans she was fired after one year as a teacher on the reservation. The old tribal women on the White Earth Reservation called her animosh, animosh, abita animosh, meaning dog, dog, or mongrel, that woman is half reservation mongrel. The mongrels would have disagreed, but Lilith Mae thought the old women meant that she was a person who loved and cared for animals. The sexual reference to her association with the mongrels on the reservation never entered her eastern-educated mind. Keeping up to this mistaken impression, she fed most of the mongrels on the reservation. She was fired not because of her relationships with the mongrels, but because of her rumored relationships with several members of the tribe during an education conference out of state. More than her time with married men and mongrels she was disliked and mistrusted because she spoke in passionless contradictions about traditional tribal culture, evidence of which escaped her on the reservation, asked stupid questions about reservation people and ceremonies, and expressed more love for animals than for the children she was hired to teach. She seemed to be above racism, or below discrimination, because she had not discovered in her experiences that human color made a difference at tables around the world. She boasted that she had sat with the best from all colors. Tribal children, whatever color, she once told a friend, would be fine, they could even be fun to be with at times, if they were not children. The principal of the school where she taught said she was practicing to become a mouth warrior.

"Bad breath causes cancer," she announced to the other teachers on the first morning of classes. Sitting in the lunch room she pinched her nose and pointed toward several tribal children with bad teeth. "Those two over there, killers, cancer killers with their bad breath. . . . Bad breath should be covered over."

"Call a dentist," a teacher responded.

Lilith Mae, who has poorer timing than a federal bureaucrat, learned somehow to tell stories. She must have learned from the mongrels when she fed them in the back of her van after school. When the reservations go to the mongrels, Lilith Mae Farrier will become the queen of the animals.

Two summers after she was fired as a teacher, she attended a two-week wilderness survival camp for women seeking personal independence. Lilith Mae continued to survive on trite ideas, her concepts about independence floated without direction like sealed bottles out to sea.

Lilith Mae moved nearer the fire and her new friends. Half the moon slid through the pine trees. With the care of an old woman she spread her hand-woven ceremonial tribal blanket on the hard earth near the fire. In the center of the blanket, which she said she had received from a pantribal female sorcerer, there were five figures woven in an even row and circled with seven colors on a rainbow. The tubular bodies of the figures were similar, but the faces changed from a smiling child on one side to a part-animal child becoming a savage beast on the other side. The beast appeared to be a visual crossing of bears and children and reservation mongrels. The colors changed with the features and expressions from white and cool blue to the beast in black and harsh blood red. Next she unrolled a quilt decorated with constellations and androgynous celestial human and animal signs. Lilith Mae protected herself during sleep from evil and erotic hostilities, she said. She slept with her head over the animals and children and under the quilted zodiacal constellation of pisces. She touched the four stars in her birth sign and walked across the heavens with her fingers while she told stories about teaching on the White Earth Reservation.

"Bad breath causes cancer," she said again and again. She repeated the sentence in place of a preface to her stories.

"The tribal women made fun of me. For two years they made fun of me, calling me abita animosh, half dog, the woman who makes love with dogs and then telling me it meant I was a person who was kind to dogs and loved to feed them. The tribal women made a fool of me on purpose, the dogs were more sensitive than were the people there.

"They made a fool out of me for a whole year and I will never forget that. Never. They made a fool of me just like my stepfather did when I was eight years old. He took me on a camping trip and told me that all fathers and daughters share a secret and then he did things to me. . . . It was just awful, awful, but I never could keep a secret. Never. That much is a good thing for me because I told my mother when we got back to the house. We were sitting at the dinner table, my mother and stepfather and two older brothers, when I told them all in vivid detail what had happened. My brothers snickered and looked into their laps. Stepfather choked on a mouthful of meat. His neck and cheeks twitched while he told me not to talk that way at the table. . . . But mother would not be fooled, she wanted to know more. No woman should be fooled. She turned red, so red she began to perspire. Then she began to whine like a frightened animal. She shivered until her whine turned into rage. First she threw things at him and then she threw him out of the house. He never knew what hit him, and all at dinner. Later mother joined a group of twice-divorced women who were told to find useful things to do in the community. What mother did, with us too, was help a group of bad-smelling radical Indians who wanted to take over the Bureau of Indian Affairs with force. Those were the days when we marched and marched all over town for tribal liberation and other things. We had too many Indians in the house. They were all over the place and stayed too long, but mother was getting the attention she needed then. She had men waiting in line in the living room. The Indians told me stories, some of them I never understood, especially the ones about drinking and treaties, but they were funny people. Too bad they smelled so bad, too much on the bad breath. Must have been from all the garbage they ate, junk food three times or more a day. Mother found them easy to cook for, she just sent them out for more junk food when they were hungry.

"Bad breath causes cancer. . . . I am just fine now. I finished college and went to work on the reservation teaching in an experimental school and the women there made a fool out of me. The reservation was nothing like those radicals said it would be like though, nothing like their words. I thought it would be a place of kindness and good feelings, sort of a paradise like the words, with animals and nature, but it was a place of tricks and hostilities.

"Abita animosh, abita animosh, half dog, they shouted to me when I fed the dogs. Abita animosh and then they all laughed at me. I though they were amusing people and loved me for what I was doing there for the children, but nobody cared for me. I had no idea they were evil and laughing at me because I had not learned the tribal language they spoke, but after all, not many of them spoke it either.

"Of course, you know about reservation mongrels. I started feeding two or three mutts at first. The dogs hung around the school to be with the kids. It was hard sometimes to tell the dogs and kids apart, but I must say I like best the kids who were more like the mongrels. They were more friendly in a kind of animal way, if you know what I mean. I was living in the teacher house right across the road and it became a habit for the dogs to wait to be fed there. I fed two or three school mongrels, at first, when school was out in the afternoon. As the weeks passed, more and more dogs came to school with the kids and waited after school was out to be fed. It was plain and simple that it was getting out of hand when two dozen dogs were hanging around my house waiting and whining to be fed every afternoon. So I hit on the idea of filling the back of my travel van with dog food and driving around the reservation feeding the dogs. I would drive up, ring a small dinner bell I found at an antique sale, and then lower the ramp from the rear doors of my van so the dogs could walk up and in to eat. And they sure did eat. It became an expensive ritual, a new tribal ceremonial, and a full-time job after teaching all day, just feeding all those hungry reservation mongrels. But the animals loved me for it, and in the next world when I come back as a dog, they will remember. Some of them will come back as humans then and treat me well, as I did them in this lifetime.

"The tribal women shouted at me when I drove up, abita animosh, and then they held their swaying stomachs in laughter. They laughed all the time while the dogs ran up the ramp into the back of my van to be fed. They laughed and all the time I thought they were thanking me in good humor for being so generous to their goddamn reservation mongrels. Those women must have thought I was making love with all those dogs in the back of my van. For a whole school year they made a fool of me at my feeding stops when I rang the dinner bell for the mongrels.

"Ding ding ding ding ding dingal dingaling. There were two boxers, never did like boxers, that I would not permit to eat out of my van.

I cursed them. I hated them because they reminded me of my stepfather. His square jaw and all. I hated them because they expected me
to feed them. I would have nothing to do with them. No boxer stepfather would eat out of the back of my van, ever. But they followed
me everywhere and kept on begging for food. They never ate but
they never stopped trying. The boxers were the only dogs I refused
to feed on the reservation. The only two, and now like a noose around
my neck I am leashed to them forever . . . forever. What ever
happened to innocence, the first recess in school, the first secrets?

"Where are the boxers now?" a woman asked.

"I put them to sleep," responded Lilith Mae.

The women looked at each other around the fire.

"Where was I now? Listen to the last part which has some humor
even though I was run off the reservation in humiliation. But then
a fool is never at home. Run off the rotten reservation. Those bastards. Nothing worth living for there now. It was the best thing that
ever happened to me though. I might still be there taking all that
crap in again, year after year trying to believe something about reservations that can never be believed for real. Taking in all that idealistic shit about the humble people so close to mother earth. Close to
the ass of mother earth. Nothing honest about those reservation
people who came into my hotel room at the education conference
and wanted my body, and more than once. The dogs never did that.
I could have appreciated the attention, but they were drunked up
and three is a bit much for me. I was willing until they told me
about what abita animosh meant, and then they made jokes about
me doing it with all those mongrels in the back of my van, they
wanted to do the same thing. . . . Enough of that now, the point
is that their wives found out and blamed me for what they did or
did not do to me. The climate turned bad and there was nothing
to do but leave the school, enough of them, I said, and decided to
leave to save my self-respect as a white person. So I hit the road. I
climbed into the cab, started the engine, turned the van around,
gave the women the finger and roared out of the schoolyard in a
cloud of dust.

"But leaving things is never easy. The dogs saw me leaving and thought that it was time for them to eat again, so they all came out to the road and ran after the van. Little did they know that I was leaving the reservation for good. Hundreds of mongrels were running after me by the time I reached the highway leading off the reservation. The reservation would never have been the same if all the mongrels had followed me off for good. It made me sad seeing all those dogs who believed in me, hundreds of yelping mongrels running after me, no one else worried about my leaving, the kids never said a thing, nothing from the people there, nothing mind you, they just made fun of me, but all those dogs who trusted and appreciated me said good-bye as they ran. They never made fun of me. It made me sad and I was crying as I drove away.

"One by one the mongrels dropped off the chase until only the two boxers were running behind the van. They must have run more than ten miles, their tongues were flopping as they ran, and they looked so tired. I was watching them from the rear-view mirror. So I stopped and let them in the back to eat and rest. I was still crying and lonely and those two boxers were so grateful after all those months when I shunned them, so grateful to eat, that they would not leave the van after they ate. In time they learned how to take care of me, you know what I mean, but I still, or did until I put them asleep, hate them because they did remind me of my step-father every time I looked at them. Boxers are not really dogs though, you know, no one would have a dog that looked like that. Since then I found out that there are very few boxers on reservations. They remind too many people of someone they hate, I suppose. Indian agents, stepfathers, someone. . . ."

> The flaming logs burned down to ashes.
> The women closed their eyes on more stories.
> Lilith Mae counted her stars into sleep.

MOTHER EARTH MAN
AND PARADISE FLIES

Thin ribbons of cloud unfurled over the setting sun near Mille Lacs Lake on the Mille Lacs Indian Reservation. Summer colors rippled on the lake. Near the new tribal marina hundreds of black flies were poised on the boat landing. Their master was singing to the water spirits.

"Our women were poisoned part white," wailed Zebulon Matchi Makwa down to the dock through the pale poplar and pine part drunk on reservation wine. "Part peeled at night ho ho ho ho buried deep down where the dead turn around and around. . . ."

Tame deer waited near the salt blocks.

Fishermen cast their lines and lures near shore.

"Our women were poisoned part white. . . ."

"His mother married a mountain bear," said an old tribal man to his toothless woman. She covered her mouth with her small hands to hide her good humor. Matchi Makwa, translated in white tongues as "evil bear," had fallen, face and shoulders first, from the tribal dock into the muck and shallow water weeds near shore.

"Our women were poisoned part white. . . ."

"He never tells on tribal bears," whispered the old man through a small round mouth. "Makwa, sure enough, has the bear name, but he never talked with bears because he has been taken too much with witching words and evil from the sorcerers in the cities."

"Our women were poisoned part white . . . too much," he wailed over and over on his stout tongue as he pushed through the reeds in shallow water toward shore. He stumbled twice in the proud reeds. The flies were down with him. He smiled, his teeth shining through the dark blue muck on the side of his round face, and stopped in the reeds to drink from his bottle of cheap red wine.

The old woman covered her mouth and laughed.

Matchi Makwa moaned ho ho ho ho onshore.

"The mountain bears brought this one home to the reservation," his mother exclaimed at his birth when she first saw the dark bear hair on his shoulders and back. She did not mean that she had conceived her fourth son with a bear, spiritual or otherwise, but once said and laughed into memories, she became the new woman in the old tribal stories who married a bear and took up the smell. Her human husband, the fisherman on the prairie with his cheeks scarred from fishhooks, laughed himself into the posture of a bear and ho ho hummed in a deep voice once or twice, but then he lost his tribal time in good humor and turned to forgetting while he drank too much wine.

Matchi Makwa was born under a new moon on the Turtle Mountain Reservation in North Dakota. When the white man asked him *where* was he born on the reservation, he said "on a crossroads in the dirt. . . . Or what was the name of that sacred crossing on the reservation." His is not a sacred tribal name in or out of translation, but the name he took from his friends at the Flandreau Indian School in South Dakota. There, boarded before he was eight, he distinguished himself with words and wine. School officials presented him with his first name.

"Zebulon, from biblical literature and for the famous military officer and explorer Zebulon Pike . . . and because we know of no one else on the reservation who is so named . . . Zebulon Bad Bear," said the officials at the school.

Zebulon could recite dozens of chapters and verses from the covenants of the Old Testament. He could speak longer than three women at a funeral for a distant cousin and with more unusual words than an unctuous conflux of inexorable and contentious polemicists. With a deep smile, a smile so deep it can turn time around, Matchi Makwa could substitute three obscure words for one simple expression. He made more sense when he was drunk, so his friends poured him cheap wine at night hoping he would run on common words. He thought he was obsessed with words and possessed with voices that spoke through him like missionaries. While holding discussions in his mind with several voices he could hear himself speaking to the various voices.

"Who talks through you now?" a tribal friend asked.

"What if the voice in me is white?"

"Better call the bureau for a new lease."

"But my ears are tribal. . . . What I hear is tribal, but it is not the same as the voices in me," said Matchi Makwa, spitting on an anthill in a crack on the cement sidewalk. His focus was perfect, casual but direct, and in nine spits between words and phrases he flooded the ant tunnels.

"You spit like a woman," said a friend.

"Stereotropic expectoration. . . . Not *like* a woman would if she could," responded Matchi Makwa, spitting three times again on a new anthill farther down the sidewalk. "Expectoration is the last metamasculine expression in passive double-binding cultures of parafeminist ideologies."

Matchi Makwa used his parapower over words and focused the white voices in him to win scholarships to attend college. He studied languages and linguistics and then taught in rural and reservation public schools. White educators were pleased to hear him tell his stories.

Faculties and students expressed respect for his mind but not for the odor from his breath and flesh. No school board asked him to teach a second year. He had the breath of summer bears and the unctuous odor from multiple viscous flesh oils and salts that attracted thousands of flies. Flies from the cafeteria and the locker room found him in the morning at his public school desk and celebrated the stench on his unwashed flesh. He was a fine teller of stories, and in the beginning at least, when he could not spit because he was in the classroom, he would catch flies in his hands and drop their dead bodies in a pile on his desk while he lectured. The students gave him several names: Doctor Bear, China Res, meaning China Reservation, in reference to the program to kill flies in China, the Indian Fly Trap, Bear Face, and Mother Earth Man. The flies loved him too, a gesture in flight that he did not appreciate at first. The flies seemed ecstatic in the stout hands of death.

"Tell about the word wars again Doctor Bear," said a senior student. The teacher bear shivered with pleasure at the thought of telling stories while he caught flies.

"Tell us again Mother Earth Man."

"Saint Louis Bearheart wrote a strange book about tribal pilgrims and their grave reports from the word wars," said Matchi Makwa, the Mother Earth Man, leaning back in his chair. "Last week I told you about the scolioma moths and the tribal pilgrims passing through groups of people with birth defects and cancer deformities. When the petroleum was gone, the government took back the trees on reservations, and when the governments failed, people formed new families based not on economic or material values, or the lack thereof, but based on their weaknesses and disabilities . . . weaknesses as the bottom-line factor in identities.

"Now let me tell you about the tribal pilgrims at the Bioavaricious Regional Word Hospital in Kansas," he began, snatching flies in flight with both hands and piling their bodies on his desk.

"Congress had at last agreed on what was causing social problems and crime. Language and words, grammar and conversations caused all the problems in the nation, the lawmakers asserted, and moved to create several regional word hospitals to take a good long and hard look at language. The government discovered that there was something wrong with talking, so said the futurist facilitators. The breakdown in traditional families was a breakdown in communication. . . . This bogus awareness caused our elected officials to create word hospitals.

"The tribal pilgrims from woodland reservations were at a loss for words to express their wonder at the creation of a word hospital to diagnose and treat common babble. One of the pilgrims said, when he entered the laboratories of the word hospital, 'words cannot describe the feeling that our language is a labor of love against which we rise up and prevail in glorious voices of pride and speak about nothing with such pleasure.' His words were applauded. 'Truer words were never spoken,' another pilgrim mocked.

"The government word doctors were known as numbers, so as to keep things straight in their heads. Three, his name, explained that 'at this hospital we find tongues in trees, books in brooks, phrases from the mouths of fish, oral literatures on the wings of insects, sermons in stone, good words here and there, words are all things to all people,' and even added that machines have their own language. The pilgrims asked him what he was talking about because tribal people have known that since the beginning of words.

"What is the good word?" someone asked.

"The tribal pilgrims, wandering from the woodland to the desert for the winter, were escorted to a large room in the word hospital where the central computers were housed. Each machine had a personal name while the word doctors, the humans, had number names. Seven, a tall woman, explained the function of Marion, a dianoetic chromatic encoder, to the tribal pilgrims. 'Simplified then, words are given color values,' said the seven woman, 'such as red for hot words and cool blue for other words. Each word is entered in the language of color, chromatic meaning is associated with other words in our experience.' One of the pilgrims asked number seven who would care about color words when communication was breaking down down down? Seven defended her work. 'If nothing else, people can *feel* when words have and do not have meaning. . . . For example, several thousand lines of color-coded free verse has been turned over to government intelligence organizations. It was like a field trip into color metaphors. We have also encoded the speeches and writings of radical organizers and terrorists. We have studied the possessive pronouns and paradoxical verbs of Dennis Banks. Remember him? He was one of the leaders of the American Indian Movement,' she said, nodding to numbers nineteen and four who joined the group in the computer room. 'We have also studied the writings of Patricia Hearst and the speeches of Bertrand Cellanoid, the racist labor organizer. The last chromatic studies were made on the words of Charles Manson,' doctor seven explained. 'But the machine stopped in confusion on this, one of his messages from prison: *dreamers dreaming dreams of dreams dreaming dreamers.* The machine choked up on his words.' When the word doctors finished their studies, after several internal word wars between the word wards in the hospital, the language had changed. The tribal pilgrims thought the word hospitals might have been modeled after the Bureau of Indian Affairs.

"The moral of this story about the word wars is that colors make more sense than words," Matchi Makwa explained. "Catching colors for words is as futile as measuring the meaning of the universe in a conversation on a late night television talk show. . . . Creative writers find words in colors, soaring birds, flowers in the sun, wine at night. The speaker is not the center of the word world because words were on the earth before the talkers and tellers.

"N. Scott Momaday, old romancioso Momaday, remember him," said Matchi Makwa, "he wrote that the 'word did not come into being, but it *was*. It did not break upon the silence, but it *was older than the silence and the silence was made of it.*' He was thinking about the oral tradition and the telling of stories, like this one, when he wrote that. Silence and wind and water sounds were here before birds and fish. The birds knew how to sing from the wind that shaped their wings in flight. Like fish out of water, white people speak words out of meaning. No wonder the white world needed word hospitals. . . .

"Dozens died during the word wars."

"Down under Mother Earth Man," his students chanted.

Matchi Makwa never missed a conference when he was a teacher and administrator in tribal education. He became known in tribal circles as the "conference savage" or the "nomadic committee bear." He could not remember one conference from the other. The women were the same to him and he told the same stories to stay alive on the road. He ate and drank and slept with white women using funds from foundations and various government agencies. Dozens of idealistic and romantic white women returned from numerous conferences burdened with reservation war stories, and one summer with a case of crabs from the bear.

Matchi Makwa was shunned at the conferences by most of his friends, notwithstanding his good humor and stories, when he stopped washing his clothes and flesh. He was never obsessed with cleanliness but once, when the airline lost his luggage, he let himself go in the same clothes for a week. Not washing saved water and time. The old bear was pleased with the smell of his own flesh. His friends noticed, but did not tell, that from month to month he wore the same clothes, three shirts and two pair of double-knit trousers, with the same wine stains from previous conferences. When it came to clothes and flesh odors there were few tacit tribal historians.

The Earth Mother Man had an overpowering stench which caused his friends to stand back at least ten feet when he told his stories, when he praised his women. People avoided him on elevators and in small rooms. Matchi Makwa smelled so bad that his friends who had known him for several years would not sit with him during meals. He attracted flies; some friends argued that several determined generations of reservation flies followed him from conference to conference.

"Flies are but metaphors," said Matchi Makwa in casual defense of his attractive stench. "Birds and even some animals eat them, at one place in the food chain flies are delicacies, so what can be so evil about flies? Flies have even been good friends."

"White Earth Reservation flies, perhaps?"

"Mixedblood flies," said another friend.

"Fourth generation Red Lakers."

"How could a woman stand his smell in bed?"

"His women must not breath during sex."

"Clean white women need his smell to overcome."

"The foul bear racism test," said another friend.

"Blondes seem to like him best."

"No sense of smell."

"Tribal women shun him on the reservation."

"But tribal women hate all men."

"What difference does a little smell make?"

Matchi Makwa had taken over a blonde singer, a piano, and a microphone in a hotel bar in Albuquerque during an annual conference of the National Indian Education Association. At first the blonde was embarrassed, pinching her thin northern nose and swishing at the flies, but when she touched the bear and listened to his stories she came into his personal power.

Even the flies listened to his stories.

"There was an old tribal man who attended all the reservation meetings with the forward observers and the landing parties during the beginning of the war on poverty. He sat in back of the room week after week listening and learning war words and the rules of order. Then one night in the spring, unable to hold back his need to speak, he stood up, wagged his hands at the chairman, and said: 'I was sittin' here from the beginning of this dumb war on the poor, where is the poor? It the poor bad? Where? The words about his war is too much talk. Now listen to me, I want to make this commotion. . . .' The people at the meeting, those planning strategic sorties against the poor, to help the poor, laughed and then the chairman ruled that the old tribal man was out of order. The old man could not now make a 'commotion or a motion,' the chairman explained in slow white government diction. The old man would not sit down. 'What about this order here, what order is this out of order?' the old man asked, wagging his hand at the chairman. 'I represent those remarks,' he said walking toward the front of the room. The people laughed again until the meeting was ended, but the old man did not leave. 'Good night general white face, good night private mixedbloods, good night, good night,' the old man chanted from the front of the room. He took the place of the chairman and looked back at himself in the back of the room, where he had been sitting for weeks. 'You are out of order back there old man, come up here and get your shoes in order. . . . Get your trees and summer clouds in order old timer,' he said, talking to the memories of the people in the back of the room until the lights were turned out."

The blonde touched him when she laughed.

The bear motioned with his lips.

Black flies circled and circled over their heads.

The audience applauded and pleaded for more.

"This next story takes place in Santa Fe," said Matchi Makwa, raising the microphone closer to his lips where he could whisper. "I met an old tribal titleholder from the reservation. He was a cripple, lost his leg in a drinking accident, how else, he once said, and explained that a logging train ran over him in the woods. When I first saw him he had been drinking at a lavish little adobe place up the hill in old town."

The Mother Earth Man paused to stroke the thighs of the blonde who was sitting close to him on the piano bench. He downed one more straight drink, raised the empty glass, smiled and grunted like a bear until someone brought him another.

"When the cripple left the bar he hopstumbled to the door with one hollow pant leg. A yapping little mutt, it looked like a walking wig from an old white woman, followed him and stood up inside his phantom leg.

"So I asked him what ever happened to his leg. First he said, 'nothing, it looks dressed enough to me redskin.' But when I nudged the dog out of the pant leg he told me the whole time on the accident, six views, over and over. . . . Listening as long as I could, I told him that I meant what happened to his wooden leg, not his real leg. He looked around the room and said, 'that one over there, that gentlemen in the blue suit, he bought my leg about an hour ago now. . . . . When you lose one you lose them all,' and hopped out the door.

"The leg buyer was one of them curatorial hustlers from old town who drank that flaming chartreuse and sat there with that wooden leg on the chair next to him. . . . The wooden leg was covered with signatures and travel decals from tourist traps across the nation. . . . On the outside of the leg, near the ankle was a plastic-covered identification card holder with a return address. So I asked the slicker in the blue suit how come he bought a wooden leg off the old titleholder, and he smiled back and said that the old man left his leg for a drink. . . . Real or wooden the old fool could not stop giving up his legs for drink.

"He was a brush savage, but the old town attracts interesting people with or without their legs. The titleholder knew no one would keep his leg for long, never had before, because the return postage was paid by a liberal foundation, so it said on the stump. . . . But most of the time someone would deliver his leg to him in the morning.

"Santa Fe artists once celebrated his wooden leg during the feast for the patron saint of phantoms and foolishness. His wooden leg is known in tribal drinking places across the nation. The leg bears the signatures and initials of famous writers and politicians.

"The white moral of this story is to stop drinking," said Matchi Makwa, as he rolled up the leg of his trousers, stiffened one leg, and limped around the tables where his friends were eating. "The tribal focus is to find free booze with a wooden leg." Thirteen people signed their names on his flesh before he returned to his blonde at the piano. She kissed him and read out loud the names. Someone had signed for Hubert H. Humphrey and President Jimmy Carter.

Matchi Makwa pleased his friends with his distance as much as he did with his stories. The blonde brushed her cheek on his shoulder near his arm pit. She had overcome the odor of the bear.

Matchi Makwa told one more story:

"Marvin Ironmoccasin lived in the tribal tradition of teaching stories. He was eighty-two years old when he received the first payment for a land-claim settlement with the federal government. The claim, involving the purchase of land by the federal government a century ago, or the land was taken and explained later, had been argued about for three generations. The waiting tribes were imaginative, the arguments with the federal government were legal double-crosses.

"Ironmoccasin, a man with many facial smiles, more smiles in a day than the good stories he knows, had waited on the reservation all his life for the claims payment. The waiting became a daylong way of life, an act of survival, a swelling symbolic system of aggressive beliefs, a source of hurried rumors, teaching stories, metaphors on paradise, and personal histories twilled together with cultural contention and humor.

"The tribes told white people lies about the woodland. The tribes invented names for tourists. Ironmoccasin told white people who asked that the families on one reservation were memorable because the men beat their heads on maple trees to draw the sap. 'The people we call the sappers or sap bangers have thick foreheads and soon lose their hair.' When white people talked about sappers and other tribal stories they were accused of being racists. White folks got the land, but tribal humor, well, no one can cut down tribal humor like trees.

"Ironmoccasin heard that the skins and mixedbloods down at the Bureau of Indian Affairs were passing rumors that the claims payment would be made before the end of the year. The government was working things out with the pig farmers again so the tribes could be paid in barrels of salt pork. Two years ago there was a rumor that payment would be made in frozen turkey, watermelon the year before that.

"The cash rumor came true. When the checks were delivered, Ironmoccasin told his wife and granddaughter that the first thing he planned to do with the money he got in the settlement was to buy his great grandson a new bicycle. But on the way to purchase the bicycle he met his old friends in town. It was a time to celebrate. It was a time to forget and then remember, the federal government came through with cash. All stories were toasted twice.

"When the celebration ended late on Saturday night the stores in the small reservation town were closed. The white owners refused to open until Monday morning. Determined to keep his promise, Ironmoccasin hired a driver to take him to Minneapolis, two hundred miles south, where he could buy a new bicycle for his great grandson. His promise was more important than the cost of transportation. The old paraeconomic survivor was bound with promises and unable to resist celebrations with friends.

"The next morning Ironmoccasin was asked by his friends why he had hired a driver and a car to take him all the way to the city and back again in one night. 'For a bicycle,' the old man answered. 'But why way down there?' his friends asked, knowing the reason but asking anyway. 'Because,' said Ironmoccasin without hesitation, 'bicycles are much cheaper down there.' "

The blonde no longer feared the tribes.

"Now for the moral of these stories," said Matchi Makwa holding hands with the blonde. "John Fire Lame Deer said that artists are the tribal people of the white world, 'they are called dreamers who live in the clouds, improvident people who cannot hold onto their money, people who do not want to face reality. They say the same thing about Indians. How the hell do these frog skin people know what reality is?' Lame Deer said: 'The world in which you paint a picture in your mind, a picture which shows things different from what your eyes see, that is the world from which I get my visions. . . . Indians chase the vision, white men chase the dollar,' and the dollar will do them in at the unleaded pumps," said the Earth Mother Man.

The stories ended and Matchi Makwa had his blonde.

When Clement Beaulieu opened the metal door to his government office on the reservation, Matchi Makwa was sitting and writing at his new metal desk. Beaulieu could smell his flesh when he entered the tribal administration building. He followed the stench and found the office of the bear.

When the bear looked up and saw his friend at the door, a wide smile spread across his brown round smooth face. His lips separated, his cheeks creased in three parts, his hair turned back, his eyes closed, and one thousand three hundred and seven black flies, who had been watching him write a letter to the commissioner of education, took flight in fine circles when he stood up and spread his arms in friendship. Beaulieu watched the flies, turned his head as he watched the flies circle their heads. He held his breath and embraced the stout bear.

"How can you work with all these flies?"

"What flies?"

"What flies? The old bear must be blind," said Beaulieu. "These black flies, thousands of them, circling our heads . . . look at them all. Enough of them to drive a whole block of suburban white housewives into madness."

"Flies never bother me," said Matchi Makwa.

"These flies must love you, look at them on you shoulders, in your hair, have you named them?" asked Beaulieu.

"Tribal place-names."

"What does that mean?"

"Named for the places the flies choose to wait for me," explained Matchi Makwa. "There are the hair and shoulder tribal flies, three generations now, crotch flies, finger and cheek flies, nose flies, forearm and underarm flies, five generations, all flies have dreams of paradise. . . . Could we harness their energies?"

"Your flesh is their paradise."

"None other than paradise for tribal flies," said Matchi Makwa, wagging his arms until hundreds of flies took to flight around his head.

"The monarch of black flies," said Beaulieu, swishing the flies from his ears and hair. "Do the flies see you as their master?"

"One hundred times more in compound vision."

"Do the flies bite you?" asked Beaulieu.

"Never. . . . Never kill flies and you too could have sensitive fellowship among the flies. . . . Watch now how attentive they are when I sit down. . . . See, they sit with me. We even walk and talk together. . . . They go crazy when I play basketball and work up a good sweat."

"No shit."

"Flies are like demons and darkness," said Matchi Makwa. "We must become what we fear the most to outwit evil and survive. . . . We overcome fear becoming what we fear. When we become flies, turning our being into flies, the flies are no problem. . . .

"I neither love nor hate flies," said Matchi Makwa. "This indifference frees me as the perfect warrior. I have no obligations to hate or desire or fear. . . . The same is true with women. It took me most of my life to remember that I could not be tamed and could never be mannered and civilized. . . . When we fear women, become a woman and the fear disappears like hexed warts."

"But what if we fear ourselves?" asked Beaulieu.

"Terrible thought . . . becoming ourselves."

"True enough for blondes."

"White women soon become what they fear the most," explained Matchi Makwa. Several flies rested on his cheeks and chin. "When women fear bears and flesh odors, and the tribes, I like them the most. . . . Never waste your time on those white women who have no fear or hatred . . . some are too free to hate."

"Who would believe you were the flies paradise?"

"Success comes from fear," said Matchi Makwa.

"What ever happened to the old church basement school of shame and guilt? Remember the old 'my pocket book is empty and mother earth is hurting' speeches?"

"The good old bullshit times."

"Our symbolic redress," said Beaulieu.

"High on the road to historical liberation."

"Obsessed with the past."

"But we are the past," said Matchi Makwa.

"Never mind that, where can we eat lunch?"

"At the marina. . . . I was there last night telling stories to a beautiful old woman who covered her phantom teeth with her beautiful reservation hands when she laughed," said Matchi Makwa. He threw his head back and laughed and mimicked the old woman covering her mouth. The flies crotched with him in compound vision.

"We were in love last night. . . . The old woman saw me in her memories coming down to the lake with the bears. . . . Ho ho ho ho I gave her my bear heart. . . . But her husband said bad things about me because he was a rodent with a small mouth."

"Would you drive please?"

"Because of the flies? You should fear them even more little mixedblood man," said Matchi Makwa. He held out his hands and dozens of flies landed on his palms and crawled between his fingers. "When the bear is here have no fear that the flies will follow you. . . . They love me."

"Mine is pure indifference."

On the road from the tribal administration building to the new reservation marina restaurant the flies swooped through the windows like thick black hands on a clock. Their motion in motion tested the paradox of time.

The flies shared lunch with the bear. The waitresses no longer kill flies in the restaurant because all the new flies, those from traveling generations, followed the bear home when he was finished with his meal.

Matchi Makwa the Mother Earth Man endured twelve months as an administrator in education and then moved back to the cities. The flies remembered the bear from generation to generation but did not survive the winter without him on the reservation.

THE EDIBLE MENU
AND SLOW-FOOD TRICKSTERS

 all me Ishmael," he said, while he escorted a short balding sociologist across Cedar Avenue in Minneapolis through bumper to bumper traffic. "Some years ago, never mind how long precisely, having little or no money in my purse . . ."

"Your purse? Who are you?"

"And who are you?" asked Ishmael.

"Herman Melville," the sociologist responded.

"Then you will understand . . . in my purse, and nothing particular to interest me on shore, I thought I would sail about a little and see the watery part of the world. . . . Whenever I find myself growing grim about the mouth; whenever it is a damp, drizzly November in my soul; whenever I find myself involuntarily pausing before coffin warehouses, and bringing up the rear of every funeral I meet; and especially whenever my hypos get such an upper hand on me, that it requires a strong moral principle to prevent me from deliberately stepping into the street . . . I account it high time to leave the institutional scenarios, through the middle of traffic like this, and get my ass out to sea as soon as I can. . . ."

"What see or sea is that?"

"The red sea on the Red Lake Reservation."

"Ferriferous water," said the sociologist.

Jerry Gerasimo, wearing a black beret and fake straw sandals, was waiting, as he has done at hundreds of intersections in his life, at the corner of Cedar and Riverside Avenue for the traffic control light to change when Ishmael touched him on the shoulder and said, with the smile of a tribal trickster, "follow me and you will see the best places to cross . . . corners are for women and fools."

"This is a bad corner?"

"Corners are not made for people to cross at," Ishmael explained. "Corners are for women, neat, angles and squares, where scenario designers have lines and curves meet to look neat . . . their mothers taught them to be neat. Corners are too neat and dangerous because women made them that way."

Gerasimo, who has lived and studied and taught in crammed urban centers most of his life, earning his doctorate of philosophy degree from the University of Chicago, had not settled on a safe way to cross Cedar Avenue until a tribal trickster from the reservation told him to ignore traffic control scenarios and cross streets in the middle of the block.

"How is it you know so much about traffic?"

"There are no corners on the reservation," said Ishmael as he stopped on the sidewalk in front of Annie's Parlour, a place of mirrors, slow-food cheeseburgers, and thick ice cream. Gerasimo invited him to lunch. "Some fast-food places have better food but the plastic scenarios take the fun out of eating," said the trickster, looking at himself in the mirror next to the sociologist. "More and more the world smells like waiting rooms, elevators, and the front seats of new cars. The people who eat in fast-food scenarios are ingesting feminist ideologies, because the whole neat and clean plastic time-saving thing was done for women. . . . So I breathe much better now in slow-food places, with good human dust and relaxed flies."

"Who *are* you?"

"The trees are tossing like ponies," said Ishmael.

Ishmael, which is not his birth name or his sacred tribal name, but the name he tells over and over in spite of unusual demands of law enforcement officers, was born in the spring in an ice fishing house—the same place where he was conceived—while the ice was breaking. One week later, mother and her ninth child, fifth son, would have dropped through the ice with the house. Ishmael, born without certification, came into the world cold but with the slim smile of a trickster. He was first known as Kagobiwe, porcupine quill, the translated name of his father whom he has never known. At mission school on the reservation he was named Noname Kagobiwe, a bristling wild child in a wild place. Some said he was wild because his father was a traveling tribal clown who tricked his mother into summer sex under the whole moon in a fish house. He faced the moon and said his face was the moon. Whole moons and trickeries are not uncommon on reservations.

Noname has lusted for women from the time he was seven, four in his telling, and had sex with a distant cousin when he was eleven, six in his telling, and makes the woman a nun. He wrote "face the moon" on walls and posts and boats on the reservation.

Noname was too wild for most reservation people. He was nine, two years before his first sex experience, when the federal government announced that new homes would be built first for those who were without housing. Noname set fires in selected shacks and wickiups to get the old tribal women into new buildings. In the best tradition of the balancing trickster he would note the habits of those whose houses he had marked to burn to be certain no one was at home when he started his fires. He used cedar and kerosene, a ceremonial mixture of the old and the new. On one occasion an old woman who had wheeled down to the local homebound drinking port for the evening was told, while she raised the third can of red pine gin to her trembling lips, that her house was in flames. "Minnie, Minnie, your house is burning down for a new one," the children chanted. "Never mind now," she said with a toothless grin. Setting the can aside and turning from the table, she smiled at the children. Then she stood and faced the children who had brought her the news about her house burning and said; "Never mind there, because we got the good key right here." She laughed and slapped her stomach. "The key is right here," she said, doubled over in laughter, "right here," slapping her stomach again and again.

"What does that mean?" asked Gerasimo.

"The word has power and there are no corners and no locks on the reservation, except the white places," said Ishmael. "The old woman never owned a lock but in good humor she sometimes carried a bundle of keys around like the government people."

"I suppose people never steal there."

"People steal on reservations, or borrow things, but locking things up makes it worse," Ishamel explained. "People who lock things up cannot be trusted because the government locks up everything . . . the old woman lived to be more than a hundred in her old house. She refused the new houses, so with the help of the missionaries the federals built her a new old house like the one that burned."

"What does it mean to lock something or someone in somewhere?" Gerasimo asked himself, spreading one finger over his lips and pulling the hairs on his moustache. "The expectation is a contradiction. . . . Listen, things locked up should stay the same, static, unused, but people change when they are locked up. . . . Where is the humor?"

"You speak like an animal on the run," said Ishamel, watching Gerasimo in the mirror at the end of their table. "The first surprise is humor."

"The last surprise is death," said Gerasimo.

"Tricksters laughing into death."

Federal officials called the fire setter the "apocalyptic optimist," but, notwithstanding their secret watches and conspiratorial investigation, no one was named or blamed for setting the fires. The federals doubted that a tribal person would be ambitious enough to plan so many fires, and to do so without burning his fingers in the act.

Ishmael was an elusive trickster. His mother worried about him when being worried was the best scenario for survival. The missionaries were impressed but did not increase their dollar contributions. The celibate patriarch of the church listened in sacred time, forgave and blessed her children, and then gave her wild fish-house son the name Ishmael. "And he will be a wild man; his hand will be against every man, and every man's hand against him; and he shall dwell in the presence of all his brethren," said the priest, quoting from *Genesis*.

"Slow foods smell better," said Ishmael, opening and closing his cheeseburger like a clam. "The smell of reservations. . . . Listen, flies even pass up the fast foods."

"Smells better than what?" asked Gerasimo.

"Better than bloated river hogs."

"But food is not what it is when we see it," said Gerasimo. "Our eyes, what we perceive on the plate, the arrangement and visual memories, the picture, this is not what our stomachs will know. . . . The test is what passes through us in good form."

"Ideologies pass in good form."

"And some people eat what comes to them in words, advertisements, as if their bodies were concepts. . . . We use our minds when our stomachs should do the talking. . . . Or is it the walking?" asked Gerasimo.

Ishmael nibbles when he eats. He has the face of a deer but eats like a squirrel. He nibbles around his cheeseburger in a perfect circle, down to the last crumb. His silver and copper bracelets, with the usual pantribal turquoise amulets, slip and tick between his elbows and wrists when he raises and lowers his food or gestures in speech.

"There is a new place to eat in the watercities called the Newmenu," said Ishmael, referring to the bay area and San Francisco, where he likes to travel in the winter. The coppers ticked on his wrists. "The menu at the Newmenu is edible. . . . Here now, these common skins turned ink and paper into nutritional meals. . . . No food there at any speed, the menu is the food, the whole meal, and the diners eat the pictures and words. The printed word and picture meals are better balanced than some real food. . . ."

"Is there a take-out service?" asked Gerasimo.

"The common skins have outwitted the stomach."

"Common skins?"

"White people, white people," explained Ishmael. "The common skins, in contrast to the rare earth skins, the people of human dust, the common skins outwit themselves into thinking that nature can be outwitted."

"Where are the rare skins when we need them?"

"Crossing in the middle of the block."

"Outwitted by nature?" asked Gerasimo, winking.

"Outwitted by nature? Of course," responded Ishmael, "but seldom outwitted by evil or trapped in one-act terminal scenarios without surprises. Common skins are never even sure when they are dead."

"Children control the world with their imagination and then plan their surprises right into unreal worlds as adults," said Gerasimo, first showing his clean white teeth and then thumping two fingers on his right temple as if he were saluting, or pounding, the content of his questions and consciousness into verbal forms. "From doll houses to franchised fast foods in the same dull dreams. . . . Scenarios are the substitutions of trauma for drama."

"You have a fine lecture voice," said Ishmael.

"The government speaks well of you too."

"Ideologies become the scenarios for what the common skins fear the most, the fear of being," said Ishmael. "Living and being, so the scenarios are plans for having and owning. . . ."

"Sonofabith. . . . Who are you?" asked Gerasimo, lisping.

"Call me Ishmael. . . ."

"Never mind that now Billy Budd. . . . But tell me this," said Gerasimo, showing his teeth again like an animal nibbling at the wind, "as a rare earth skin, as you say, and you do have rare skin indeed, but look," he emphasized, extending his short forearms, "we could both be rare skins from the ancient worlds, what is the difference between scenarios and rituals?"

"Rituals are celebrations," said Ishmael.

"Scenarios are not?"

"Scenarios are planned not celebrated," said Ishmael. "Rare skins celebrate the past into sacred time and places, not the chicken-feather fakeries and old moccasin walking and talking social medicine shows, but words as states of being on the road to paradise."

"What does *that* mean?"

"The government speaks well of you too."

"You talk like an anthro apologist," said Gerasimo.

"Scenarios are planned not celebrated. . . ."

"You already said that. . . . And rituals celebrate the known and the unknown, even the foreknowable. . . . The conscious and the unconscious through time and space, not a plan to inhibit surprises and the unknown. There are no mysteries in scenarios."

"Eating fast foods and waiting on the corner to cross with the right light is a scenario on the road to evil," said Ishmael, smiling again in the mirror with the tricksters. The coppers and silvers ticked down his arm. "Crossing in the middle of the block is a ritual. . . . Too much planning at the corners. Women did it to us, women make people show and tell and cross at corners close to their edges."

"What are you looking at?"

"The tricksters," said Ishmael.

"Where?"

"In the mirror there."

Ishmael tells on the weather in metaphors. His realities and memories are expressed in the visual language of weather and changing seasons. He moves his heart with wind and rain, and speaks through the images of birds and animals about time and temperature. Even while he was in prison he told the temperature in images and descriptions rather than in abstract numbers and quantities. His was not a world of mind over perspiration, he explained. Ishmael told those who pretended to listen that even Anders Celsius, the Swedish astronomer, had feelings about the temperature before his temperature scale had meaning.

Ishmael explains that weather is visual and sensual but not an abstract scenario separation in numbers. "The weather is not the mind over perspiration."

"Cold enough to stop the wings on dragonflies. . . . Tell the geese to land before the sun sets. . . . Warm as the breath of bears. . . . Too warm to move the flies from the screen door. . . . The ice is as thin as isinglass this morning."

The prison psychiatrist, however, being a person who views scenarios as normal measures of realities, diagnoses visual weather reports as a form of social dissociation. "The temperature, to this incarcerated subject," the psychiatrist wrote in his notes, is not the temperature at all, but a delusion, a dream image. . . . Subject, a six-foot handsome buck who has not recognized the seriousness of his crime, refuses to accept common social measures. . . . Conclusions: undeveloped social controls and arrested perceptions of common realities."

Ishmael was immature, what else could a trickster be in the world of scenarios, but not about the weather and fast-food eating places. He suffered from retarded social controls in the new urban world, on street corners in the presence of common-skinned women, for example. In less than two weeks time, while he was home on leave from the service, he burglarized a store, completing a first-degree scenario at night while someone was there, which then carried a life sentence upon conviction. He was also arrested on a rape charge, though the white woman invited him to her apartment, where, she testified, he took valuables from her purse. Ishmael explained to the public prosecutor that the woman was not pleased because "all I wanted was sex and all she wanted to do was walk around and be told that she was loved. . . . Word love, you know what I mean?" The prosecutor smiled at the trickster, but he was worried about reelection, so he bargained with the rare skin, plead guilty, guilty, as charged and we can arrange a reduction in sentence time. Time was never explained. Ishmael, who smiled at the judge, was sentenced to prison for life, on the first-degree burglary charge, and forty years for rape, to be served consecutively. The prosecutor won reelection.

But Ishmael, praising all surprises, was at sea again in less than six months. He worked up a case of serious conflicting scenarios while in prison which required treatment at the local word and head hospital. Once there, he called up the weather and drifted home to the reservation. Federal officers found him floating in a canoe in the middle of his red sea on the reservation. Ishmael floated in freedom for four days and nights, while the officers waited on shore, and then on the fifth night a severe storm blew the canoe to shore near the tribal village of Ponemah. He was returned to prison. On the road, sitting in the back seat in handcuffs, Ishmael explained his values to the officers, the differences between freedom and escape. "Sailing is freedom, the sea is free. . . . Prison is a scenario, an old-world mind fuck. Bored women made prisons. . . . The world could suffer heart failure in too many scenarios."

Ishmael was convicted for escape, charges he never argued or denied. Freedom is obvious, he told the prosecutor, emphasizing the word freedom, rather than escape. He continued serving his sentences until a mixedblood social worker celebrated his views on the world and recommended a special release. The parole board turned him out, but Ishmael, ho humming his fine freedom, crossed at the middle of the block too often in violation of his parole and was returned to prison for several more years. It was then that he learned how to outwit evil and feminist scenarios.

"Was the middle of the block, the figurative middle, worth the round trip to prison?" asked Gerasimo, pinching his nose and twirling single hairs from his beard. His face wrinkled when he listened.

"Metaphors are not quantities," Ishmael responded. "The mind weather was fine, but I was slow to learn about scenarios. We all rappel in the spring like inchworms down the elmslides and some lose their ropes. . . . The scenarios begin with those who see us falling in freedom and fear for their secure ropes."

"Falling as perfect warriors."

When the two had finished their meal, Ishmael brushed the table clean, wiped his slender dark hands, pulled out a deck of plastic cards from his pocket, and dealt two hands of five cards face down.

"Who are these women?" asked Gerasimo as he picked up the cards one at a time and touched the plastic faces. "What game are we playing now?" The cards were color photographs of naked women.

"These are my women."

"Your women?" asked Gerasimo.

"I have had sex with all of them," said Ishmael, turning his cards over and smiling at himself in the mirror. "Which one would you like tonight in my deck?"

"You do have a full deck."

"These are the best."

"But these are the same faces that are on the cards sold in porn shops," said Gerasimo, examining the five nude bodies in his right hand. "These are your word women."

"Vision women," said Ishmael.

"Fine bodies, but what are you telling me, selling me, about these women? . . . What is your thing about women?" asked Gerasimo without looking up from his hand.

"I made them all in prison."

"Who will ever know?"

"Women love to be told that I masturbated with them in mind," said Ishmael. "Women are never warriors. . . . Their faces and bodies are scenarios, mind scenarios, prison scenarios for me. . . . Sex is a scenario and women have turned the world into mindless scenarios to get sex. . . . I made them all on the cards in prison."

"Does your mother love you?" asked Gerasimo.

"For a little sex with women, men have downed virgin forests, cut roads through the wilderness, invented cosmetics, insect killers, clothes without pockets, washing dishes without spots, smooth laxatives, plastics, various time-saving machines, and have tried to outwit nature near the grave. . . . Women have planned it all from childhood. . . . Women made all the corners, show-and-tell places, where you were waiting, and women planned all the fast-food scenarios. . . . Women want to control the last free flies from the garbage. . . ."

"But what about men and their need for power?"

"Some men are nothing but women."

"Ishmael indeed, someone did call you right."

"Warriors pursue nothing but their dreams and visions," Ishmael continued. He shuffled the deck and smiled. The coppers ticked on his arm. "Women are not free on the sea, women are never warriors. . . . These cards, the edible menu, soaring birds, these are dreams. . . . Would a warrior pursue the flesh when he can have women, all women on these cards, in his dreams, without acting out mindless scenarios?"

"Is that a question?" asked Gerasimo.

"No, an answer, but what is your question?"

"You could be the winning hand of some trickster."

TRAVELS WITH
DOCTOR GERASIMO

Artless appearances can be deceptive.

"It do not make no difference which road from this time here is taken," said the man dressed in red and blue and leaning on a rack of used tires in a cut-rate service station. He attempted to speak with formal attention to directions, but he wavered like a domestic bird on his feet and words. "That school over the hills . . . over the hills there."

"What hills?"

"Whatacallit white over those hills," he said, dragging his short stout arm, marked with crude tattoos honoring his women and the tribe, across the tires to point. He pointed with his lips too, and when he smiled, never being certain in which direction he was aimed that morning, his black eyes squeezed shut. Then he wiped his face with his hands until his cheeks slid down to their usual unsmiling place.

"Too much white water on the red roots, brother," said Beaulieu through the car window as he drove down the drive, past the pumps, sounding the station bell three times, and turned westward through the town.

Gerasimo sneezed.

There were no hills but those in the mind between the service station in Breckenridge, Minnesota and Wahpeton, North Dakota. Clement Beaulieu and Jerry Gerasimo were looking for the Wahpeton Indian School.

"Where are the hills?" asked Gerasimo.

"Everything white is over the hill," said Beaulieu.

"Whatacallit white. . . . Did you hear his formal use of double negatives?" asked Gerasimo, wiping his nose with a single tissue peeled from a blue bundle carried in his back pocket.

"Must have learned his negatives in an artless federal boarding school," said Beaulieu, driving on the bridge across the Red River and crossing the border between the two states.

"John Adair, that gentle desert anthropologist who never leaves home without his faithful hound panting less than full tongue at his side, told me at a linguistics meeting that double negatives are self correcting. . . . Do you suppose he tells nothing unimportant?"

"Nothing is not unimportant," added Gerasimo.

"Transfiguration through triple negatives," said Beaulieu.

The Wahpeton Indian School, an artless federal boarding school for tribal children, was conceived with colonial ideologies and is now administered by the Bureau of Indian Affairs.

Federal boarding schools have low reputations in tribal histories. Tribal people have not forgotten that at the same time colonial policies suppressed the expression of tribal languages and religions at boarding schools, hundred of miles from tribal homes and families, the federal government was subsidizing linguistic and anthropological research on reservations to record what was being lost under colonial duress.

"Listen to this," said Gerasimo. He was reading from a manuscript entitled *Bearheart*, an unpublished novel by Saint Louis Bearheart. "Listen to this now:

"The bear is in me now.

"Listen ha ha ha haaaa.

"Not since the darkness at federal boarding school and the writing of our book has the blood and deep voice of the bear moved in me with such power.

"We speak the secret language of bears in the darkness here, stumbling into the fourth world on twos and fours, turning underwords ha ha ha haaaa in visions. The bear is in our hearts. Shoulders tingle downhill on dreams. The darkness moves through me in ursine shivers.

"Measure most of our lives in darkness, count in silence our faces on the dawn, include service during the wars, turning out miles and miles of heirship records at small federal desks, under the slow motions of government forearms, all the while we dream about the omens and grave stories we would tell on the future of the tribes at war with words and evil. . . .

"Voices of the bear spoke through me first when the superintendent locked me in a small dark closet. For a time I moved alone through hatred and the darkness with picture memories on clouds and trees and birds. Three times as a bird before the bear opened his maw and took me into his heart. In dark fur we passed through federal school time on the winter solstice.

"Listen ha ha ha haaaa.

"I was twelve years old and had run from the school four times. The moons were whole. The assiduous government agents were waiting, waiting waiting generation after generation without fail for the defeated tribes to stop running. The agents, hired hunters for the givers of government, captured me once as *me* and three times as a *bird* and ran me back four times from the sacred cedar.

"The first time, to teach us all good lessons not to run with the tribes and good visions of inner birds and animals, the agents forced me to wash floors and clean toilets for two months.

"The second time back, from the sixth grade then, being in the vision of a cedar waxwing, the cruel and mawkish federal teachers pushed me naked into the classrooms, me and the bird in me, and whipped us for our avian dreams.

"The third time back as a blue heron from the shallow rivers we were led on a leash to the classrooms and chained at night to a pole in the cowshed.

"We survived as birds and animals because we were never known as humans. Evil teachers who are you hiding from now? Did you ever hear our woodland calls and whistles? We dreamed free from our chains.

"The fourth time back to school, listen now in this darkness, handcuffed and bruised, the last time as a bird, we learned to outlive and outwit government evil. The superindendent of the boarding school, the wishwash deceiver, pushed and punched us into a dark windowless room near his office. There, with his stiff angular hands, he wore three copper bracelets to hold back the deformities that crawl through evil bodies, he forced us to kneel at a faldstool and told us he would open the door and feed us when he could hear us begging forgiveness in a loud and constant voice. His bull terrier snapped at the bottoms of our bare feet. We were silent for six nights. Time was darkness then.

"Through the small ventilator hole near the ceiling of the tall room, twice as tall as it was wide, we could hear the harsh strained voices of the superintendent and his fools. We could smell the bitter poison from his thin imported cigars. The bird in me was tired and weak without water space. . . ."

Gerasimo stopped reading and sneezed.

"Who is the *we* in his voice?" asked Beaulieu.

"The *we* is the character and the·bird or the bear, he tells on himself from two places of consciousness," Gerasimo explained. "From his human place in the closet and from his other consciousness, his vision, his survival as a bear." He peeled two tissues from his blue bundle and wiped his nose.

"We learned how to outwit evil at the faldstool. . . . On the seventh morning in the closet we chanted woodland litanies until the superintendent heard us and thought we had been trouched at the stool. In the darkness, during our recitation, he faced us and placed his hands on our shoulders. His thin crotch smelled from urine. The bull terrier, his mood the same as his master, licked our feet. Your lesson has been learned, he said, and turned us loose. We took the darkness with us then. . . ."

"Perfect timing. . . . There is the boarding school not over the nonhill," said Beaulieu, turning right. "Should we take on darkness or the superintendent first?"

Gerasimo spoke with good humor and respect about the superintendent, telling that with or without a bull terrier he placed high on the social scale measuring bureaucratic humanism.

Colonel Whitehall, retired combat officer, superintendent of the Wahpeton Indian School greeted the two visitors at the door, offered them fresh coffee, and then returned to his conservative institutional chair behind his neat federal desk. The two visitors sat in straightback chairs facing the superintendent. He spoke about computers and the new principles in federal administration and management.

Beaulieu looked past the superintendent, northward through the double windows. Focusing on floating lumps of spring clouds the room seemed to move westward.

"Are you the writer?" asked the superintendent, referring to articles Beaulieu had written about the Bureau of Indian Affairs.

"Yes," responded Beaulieu.

Colonel Whitehall leaned back in his chair, laced his long fingers together and smiled. The room moved through the clouds in the window behind him. "We have nothing to hide here. . . . We have one of the best schools where parents are part of the program," he said.

Gerasimo told about his experiences in education and about his graduate studies in human development. Colonel Whitehall emphasized practical events and avoided abstract references or ideological discussions.

"But rather than talk about the school," the superintendent said, "you should look around for yourself. . . . Visit anywhere you like, talk with the teachers and students, and then meet me in the cafeteria for lunch and a special cultural performance by one of our young Indian students."

Tribal children swarmed the visitors when they entered the dormitories. The children touched and pulled at their clothing. "I love you all, all, all," said Gerasimo, laughing and extending his arms around five dark heads. "But leave me whole, whole, whole. . . ."

Following lunch the superintendent escorted the two visitors into a large room with a polished wooden floor. There were three folding chairs and a small table at one end of the room. A tape recorder was on the table.

"We have a surprise planned for you," said Colonel Whitehall in a cheerful voice. "This will be an example of how we encourage our students to cherish their culture. . . . There was a time, as you well know sir, when dancing was forbidden, but all that has changed now, and for the better, I must add, sir."

The superintendent was proud to introduce a twelve-year-old tribal boy to the visitors who were standing near the chairs and the tape recorder. The child smiled and Colonel Whitehall touched him on the shoulder.

"Now you can get your costume on for the dance," said the superintendent in a gentle but patronizing tone of voice.

The tribal child left the room.

"This is a special moment for him," said the superintendent, looking toward the door several times. "He has been practicing this tribal dance for several weeks now, this is his first real performance."

"What is the dance?"

"Watch him now sir," Colonel Whitehall said as he pushed a button on the tape recorder. The music started.

"What is that music?"

"The Lord's Prayer," said Colonel Whitehall.

"My God," said Beaulieu, covering his mouth.

"Bless these children," said Gerasimo.

The tribal child heard the music and danced into the room across the hardwood floor toward the visitors. He wore a simulated ceremonial headdress made from erect chicken feathers which had been stained bright yellow.

"Bless these children."

In the center of the room in front of the two visitors and the proud superintendent the tribal child danced and gestured with his hands and arms in an unusual manner.

"What do the signs mean?"

"The gestures are the words of the Lord's Prayer in Indian sign language," said Colonel Whitehall, unashamed and certain that what he had taught the child was connected in some way to the secrets of his tribal soul.

"Bless these children."

"What have you done to that child," said Beaulieu beneath his breath as he left the room in disgust. He paced up and down the hall in a rage. Blood thundered in his ears. He waited near the door for several minutes and then forced himself to return to the room where the child was dancing in chicken feathers.

The tribal child was called to please visitors and his teachers and boarding school masters, but without knowing better his foolishness. He was proud for the moment with the favors of the superintendent, but his pride was at the expense of his own tribal experiences and historical identities.

"Who will he become in yellow chicken feathers?" asked Beaulieu. The child had finished the dance, motioning with his arms to the firmament without end and then returned to his class.

"We teach him to be proud that he is an Indian," said Colonel Whitehall, pinching his nose and scratching his cheek.

"Are you proud that you are white?"

"Yes, of course."

"Did a tribal person put you in a boarding school and teach you to be a proud whitian, with rubber tomahawks and bear-claw decals, while the world around you was nonwhite?" asked Beaulieu, pacing on the hard wooden floors and lecturing in a loud voice.

Colonel Whitehall was silent.

"When will he learn that what he did for us in yellow chicken feathers had nothing to do with him or us. . . . When will he understand what a fool he became for pride offered at the end of a white tongue, sir?" asked Beaulieu.

Colonel Whitehall unplugged the tape recorder.

"You are a dream killer," said Beaulieu, holding back the rage in his voice. "You have made that child a tourist attraction, a fool in a false culture. . . . In time he will hate you and hunt you down for what you have done to him here."

Beaulieu rubbed his forehead with both hands.

Silence.

Someone opened and closed a door down the hall.

Gerasimo sneezed.

The superintendent frowned, but did not respond. He removed the reel and closed the tape recorder, folded the chairs and stacked them against the wall, neat and in order, and then wished fair weather to the two visitors. He was gentle, possessed of proper manners, not a quarrelsome person, an officer to the end.

"Remember the bears," said Gerasimo.

"Come back, sir, again," said Colonel Whitehall, standing at attention outside the building. He smiled in proper form, a credit to his federal appointment, and then turned and followed the new cement sidewalk across the prairie back to his neat office.

White Hawk and the Prairie Fun Dancers

NO REST FOR
THE GOOD SHERIFF

he Sheriff of Clay County, Vermillion, South Dakota, blew
his nose and then looked out the window in the middle of
the morning. Sheriff Arnold Nelson gives good meaning to
several agreeable and complaisant counterwords. He is real neat and
nice, from the plain prairie book of manners, clean-cut hair, but not
so agreeable about being agreeable, he argues, not this morning mister, not willing here to consent to the liberal politics and sleek law
enforcement standards. He smiles when he talks and walks and
smokes.

Sheriff Nelson seldom sits at his desk. He is on the road serving
subpoenas, listening to courtroom sermons and blather at the local
truckstops, or cooking for the inmates. The few hours a week he is
in his spare office in the courthouse, he drinks black coffee with a
spoon in the cup, angles his narrow feet over the out basket, cocks
his wooden swivel chair to the southside, the windowside, and pre-
pares to witness the changing of the leaves on the trees.

He is listening to a writer.

"Nothing cordial about the first month of spring . . . still frozen at the stumps," said Clement Beaulieu, referring to the bare trees. "March is a cruel month this year."

"The word was sleek," said the sheriff, shifting his plain plastic-framed spectacles. "No sleek law enforcement here. . . . Nothing smooth and polished like in the cities. We are what we do here, no sleek public relations."

"Then tell me now, once and for all, did someone here tape all telephone calls made by inmates from the cell house, and when you finish that answer then tell me, who were the people who threatened to kill White Hawk and how did you stop them? Is that enough for openers?" asked Beaulieu.

Sheriff Nelson was silent. He lowered his wrinkled chin and opened his lips to receive a short unfiltered cigarette. His blunt fingers and lower teeth were stained from nicotine. Except for his hair, too short, and ears and spectacle frames, he could have been the weathered face in cigarette advertisements.

He smokes in silence.

Thomas James White Hawk, handsome tribesman and premedical student at the University of South Dakota in Vermillion, had confessed to the killing of a white man and was sentenced to death in the electric chair.

The Honorable James Bandy, First Circuit Judge, cleared his throat, touched his white moustache with his middle finger, and read the final sentence: "It is the sentence and judgment of this court, and it is ordered and adjudged, that, by reason of your conviction of the crime of murder of James Yeado, you, Thomas James White Hawk, suffer death by electrocution, and may God have mercy on your soul."

The Criminal Judicial Procedure of the South Dakota Code provides that after "the execution a post mortem examination of the body of the defendant shall be made by the physicians present and they shall report in writing the result of their examination. . . .

After such post mortem examination the body of the defendant, unless claimed by some relative, shall be interred in a cemetery within the county where the penitentiary is situated, to be designated by the warden, with a sufficient quantity of quick-lime to consume such body without delay.

"No services shall in any event be held over the body of the defendant after such execution except within the wall of the penitentiary, and only in the presence of the officers and guards of said prison, the person conducting the services, and the immediate family and relatives of the deceased defendant. . . . ."

But there was more than the brutal killing of James Yeado, the amiable old jeweler, that provoked the white vengeance of a college town on the prairie. White Hawk was accused of raping Dorthea McMahan Yeado several times, while her husband was bleeding to death from two small caliber gun shot wounds.

White Hawk, with his student friend and drinking partner William Stands, entered the Yeado home at dawn, the court records revealed, on Good Friday while the couple was sleeping. Dorthea was bound and blindfolded. Her gentle husband of thirty-six years was shot twice in the chest causing massive internal bleeding. He was beaten and rolled in a carpet to die hours later in the basement of his house. The cast-iron skillet used to pound his head and face broke from the force of the blows. His blood, gathered in some strange and unnatural ritual, was placed in a pan in the oven. White Hawk was found hiding like a child in a closet in the house.

"During the whole time I was at Vermillion," White Hawk wrote in a letter following his sentence to death, "I felt that somebody should pay for what had happened to Mr. Yeado. Naturally, as I was the person who held the rifle, I felt that I should pay equally for the death of Mr. Yeado. I disregarded the circumstances of the crime completely. I knew I wasn't the same person that went into the Yeado home. I made mention of this fact to Judge Bandy, specifically . . . I never really considered the outcome of my possibly robbing Mr. Yeado's jewelry store. I was selfish enough to not care for other people's rights. Now that I think about my thoughts, I didn't actually know *what* I wanted. I was tense; I was a nervous wreck. . . .

"Because I had disgraced my name I didn't want to live with it: then I didn't anyway. I was thinking how my uncle must surely have been heart broken because of my involvement in the Yeado homicide.

"Now that this sentence has been pronounced I feel free—unburdened. But I also feel now that we, as humans, can not take our own lives whenever we feel like it. In effect that is what I had done when I pleaded guilty to premeditated murder. I felt sure of what Judge Bandy would pronounce as the sentence for my plea. In fact I had no doubts; it was something I had sensed all along.

"Tentatively, I am becoming tense again because of the reexposition of the facts. But now I feel I want to *do* something about my condition and circumstances; not just throw in the towel because of minor let downs.

"To me life is more than marriage and having money. I learned that the hard way. Humility was something I didn't have."

Vermillion is a peaceful place for most of the white people living there. University students disturb the domestic solitude from time to time, but the sowing of wild oats in town, when the wild oats and sowers are white, is taken with calmative good humor. There were many outlandish incidents, as in most towns, to remember, such as peculiar domestic exchanges between husbands, but now the residents will never forget the savage who killed their jeweler and was accused of raping his wife. It became the worst crime in collective memories.

White Hawk, once the exceptional tribesman on the narrow white road to assimilated success, was born under the sign of Taurus on the Rosebud Reservation in South Dakota, but his personal time and place in the world was never known. Calvin White Hawk, his father, who once beat his mother with a plucked chicken, moved nine times in thirteen months between the cities and the reservation. His parents died before he was twelve. When his father was killed on the reservation in an auto accident, White Hawk was placed at the Bishop Hare Mission Home in Mission, South Dakota, until Philip Zoubek, his guardian, took him to the Shattuck School in Faribault, Minnesota. Zoubek wanted him to become an outstanding athlete, perhaps a medical doctor, but his surrogate tribal child committed the most atrocious crime in town and was sentenced to death.

"He had difficulty compromising," explained Burgess Ayres, headmaster of the Shattuck School. Those who knew White Hawk became instant biographers. Some friends and teachers were censured for being apologists. The Honorable Fred Nichol, the federal district judge who presided at the trial in St. Paul of American Indian Movement leaders Dennis Banks and Russell Means, had placed White Hawk on probation several months before the homicide, for the unauthorized use of an automobile and driving it across state lines. The liberal judge, a compassionate humanist, was criticized after the fact for being too lenient with White Hawk.

For some, a few hateful drunks and white people with rancor and racial loathing, the confession to homicide and the scheduled electrocution was not punishment enough.

White Hawk had accepted the death sentence until Minneapolis attorney Douglas Hall, Clement Beaulieu, Ronald Libertus, and others, convinced him to appeal his sentence and struggle to stay alive.

"Tell me what happened, constable," Beaulieu asked again and again. He had been asking all week about the thwarted attempt to kill White Hawk while he was held in the Clay County jail in Vermillion. Sheriff Nelson admired his persistence, but revealing the bootless schemes of drunken hotheads from his own town was political suicide. He smiled but would never answer the question about monitoring and taping telephone calls to and from the jail. How could he learn to trust a liberal tribal writer from the woodland to conceal and protect his sources about the threat?

"Tell me, who were the bastards?"

Silence.

"Friends of yours?"

The radiators hissed and clanked.

Sheriff Nelson finished his second cigarette and then, shifting his gaze from the trees for a moment, he lifted his feet from the out basket, poured himself another cup of coffee, and walked to the window. He scratched his head and crotch. Nelson did not wear a uniform and with his near-bald head and large ears he did not cut an imposing law enforcement figure.

Silence.

Sheriff Nelson, standing in front of the window, began speaking in a most unusual manner. Still looking out at the trees he lowered his voice and talked to himself in the best oral tradition. He spoke from visual memory in the tradition of tribal oral literature as if the official written facts and the legal words had ended in a bad sentence.

"White Hawk was calm all the way from the closet to jail. . . . I knew the Yeados and knew the house. They were very neat people and while I was looking under the bed I saw these clothes messed up in the closet and I knew she would never leave things like that, so I went over with my gun on it and the first handful I grabbed was black hair, it was White Hawk.

"I said, 'Don't move or I'll blow your brains out,' and he said, 'I won't,' so I edged him out of the closet and we took him down. He never was a problem. On the way out of the house he said 'I didn't pull the trigger.' He was bothered by the people outside waiting to see who it was inside.

"When I got him down to the jail he said he wanted to talk to me, but I kept telling him many times that he should be talking to an attorney and he kept saying to me he didn't want one. So I had to listen. . . . No, he never did break down.

"The next day this funny bird Zoubek was down at the police

station after dark and called me at home, telling me he came all the way from Minneapolis to see Tom. I told him it wasn't visiting time, so I went down and talked to him, I wanted to know if he had been down before and given that gun to White Hawk, the one he used in the killing, and he said to me that, 'so that's the way you'll let me visit Tom,' and I told him right there that as far as I was concerned I didn't want to talk to him again. I left and got a call from his attorney that he was all shook up and I finally let him in. He's a strange bird, I could tell that right away. . . .

"Tom and I got along just fine. I think I knew him better than anyone. I lived with him for almost a year. You know, he started painting right away, he was damned good. I liked what I saw. I've got his first painting. That fellow Zoubek has all the rest of his stuff. Then he dropped painting just like that and took up electronics. And then he dropped that about the time he was seeing the psychologist and started reading sociology and psychology. . . ."

Sheriff Nelson shifted his weight from side to side as he spoke. His blue trousers were caught up on the top of his black boots. He sipped his coffee, holding the useless spoon with two fingers on the rim of the cup, and scratched his head.

"I talked a lot with him. He always wanted to talk. Stands was different, he never said much, he was more like the reservation Indian. White Hawk knew he had problems and used to say maybe if he understood himself he could help others. He exercised every day, kept in good shape. . . .

"I always fed them good. Never had any complaints. I made all the food right there in the jail. I remember the first night I came home and told my wife I had to fix comething for Tom and she gave me trouble right there. 'He doesn't have to eat,' she told me. I thought I was going to have trouble at home too. I never knew how much pressure I was under then until it was over."

White Hawk wrote the following in a date book for Saturday, January 13, 1968: "Arnie promised chicken and dumplin's but failed to come through because of a preoccupation with legal matters. . . . Not much else done."

On Sunday, January 14, 1968, White Hawk wrote the following: "Arose at 4:30 A.M. Played guitar. Listened to radio. Read 'Living Free' by Joy Adamson. Regretted that Elsa died after book was completed. . . . Much too easy for a lioness. Stayed up all night but slept all day. Have had trouble sleeping at night lately. Feel urge for tranquilizers but am resisting as much as possible."

On Monday, January 15, 1968, nothing was written in his date book. On that day White Hawk was sentenced to "suffer death by electrocution."

"White Hawk had been here about three months and had some pains," the sheriff said, still standing near the window. "The doctor finally came over and we took him to the hospital. He was there about five days. I even had trouble there, got heat from the hospital. A couple of nurses wouldn't have anything to do with him.

"He had several visitors. First the minister and his wife and then she came quite often alone. And Zoubek. Two students from the University wanted to visit and I asked Tom about it and he said he would like to see them. Then two sisters from Mission and then his girl Dotty came over and told him it was all off. She had another man. Tom blew and I told my deputy to get her the hell out of here. I wouldn't let her visit again, but I did let Tom call her a few times. We had a phone in there. When she left he busted up a wooden chair into little pieces just like that. He said bad things. "I've beat five other men for her, and I'll kill him.' I told him he had enough problems.

"On top of everything I had to worry about, those people coming from the Eagles Club, and when they were drinking you never know what they might try. . . . Someone came down here drunked up and started shooting, so I made it clear to everybody that I'd put my life on the line and start shooting back if anyone tried something. . . . I don't have to mention all the names but a few days after Tom was in jail this damned fool came charging in here and we had to throw him out . . . and I told him he better not set foot around here again. . . .

"People around here think that the Minnesota American Civil Liberties Union is trying to get White Hawk off, they don't understand, and with all this communist stuff around . . . I believe that the police are the only people who can keep the communists from taking over."

Silence.

Sheriff Nelson sighed and then turned from the window where he had been talking. "Well, so you are still sitting here, are you," he said, gesturing toward Beaulieu. "You know, you should do something to inform people around here about the real work of those civil liberties people."

"Those were fantastic stories you told there."

"What stories?" asked Sheriff Nelson.

"The ones at the window," said Beaulieu.

"I have been known to talk to myself, but I can say with a clear conscience that I have never told you anything you think you might have heard me say out the window."

"Most unusual use of the oral tradition," said Beaulieu.

DAISIE AND BEACHER
ON THE PRAIRIE

The Reverend Beacher Givens was a beached clerical fish from the new school which had slipped from the sacred heaven hook and dropped double-crossed down on the prairie where the springs were too late and the summers too humid and hot to make it possible to appreciate the back roads to ministerial paradise. Beacher landed in Nebraska and buried the secrets of his piscine prison. He smiles with dramatic care on the crippled and deformed while he passes the collection baskets around the small unnatural pond from which his contributors watch him leap and hear him speak once or twice a week. No one in his little parish has been hooked so well on the heaven hooks since the good pastor fell from grace to the prairie.

When he sermonizes, hooking his words from desperate dreams, during services and meals, worshiping over more table food than living flesh, he sees the world according to a personal water model and time scheme which records his birth as the metaphorical flood. When Beacher responds to the adolescent summons, "Man, where are you coming from?" he responds, "From the flood brother, from

134

the flood dear sister, from the fish in the flood, from mother flood."

Reverend Givens sermonizes too much over food, all food, wedding cakes, warm tomatoes, one bran muffin at a time, minerals in the water, fastfoods, mint candies, fasting on verbal space. He eats with clerical relish but poor social taste.

At drive-in restaurants Beacher chants his meal sermon into the microphone with the order. "Bless these good papaburgers from the flood, from the mother flood. . . ." The intense content of his sermons seems to shape the unnatural form of his experiences. His arms, face, hair, hands, neck and shoulders, ears and fingers, all move in sudden independent gestures, unrelated and unconnected to the meaning of his words. He is formless. During his sermons over the mount he moves like a misshaped marionette on broken fishline from heaven.

Clement Beaulieu was invited to dinner.

"So good to share our time now."

"To our time then."

"To our time and the mother flood."

Beaulieu and Givens toasted their lives and their time with sweet red wine. The three broke bread from a crisp loaf in the candlelight. Beacher seated in the chair of the patriarch served the meal from his place.

"Mother flood?" asked Beaulieu.

"Never mind now Beacher," said Daisie.

"From our mother came all this from the flood. . . . Eating the food from our mother, the first mother," Beacher chanted. "Eating our mothers here. . . ."

"This is dinner," exclaimed Daisie.

"The flood is with us now," said Beaulieu, smiling.

"Mother tastes good," said Beacher.

"Will you share the night with us?" asked Daisie.

"What does that mean?" asked Beaulieu.

"Daisie means the guest room."

Beaulieu was investigating the life of Thomas James White Hawk and had driven to the Nebraska prairie to talk with Daisie and

Beacher about their experiences with White Hawk when they visited him in the county jail before he was sentenced to death.

"Did White Hawk tell you his dreams?"

"Too often," said Beacher, "he told me he had dreams about animals . . . his dreams were suicidal."

"Not suicidal," said Daisie. She brushed back her red hair with both hands. "Tom never thought about suicide, but he did think about killing other people."

"Who would he kill now?" asked Beaulieu. "One of his teachers back on the reservation thought he had killed his guardian when he killed the jeweler."

"Not killing, but thinking the end of people," Daisie explained in mitigation. She was defensive for White Hawk. "He is too cool. . . . Too brilliant and handsome." She brushed her hair back again. Beacher turned in his chair. "You can't just tell him things, he has to understand for himself, it has to come from him. . . . He has to control everything. He has to control the world."

"Yes," said Daisie, "he has dreams about animals, but he had other dreams too, about running in a track meet and not being able to run fast enough. . . . He dreamed also about the walls closing in on him in the cell and about his parents."

White Hawk wrote this, three months following the death sentence, about two of his dreams: "While I was at Vermillion, the county jail that is, I dreamed of my mother and father.

"I was laying on the cell bunk on my back and went to sleep. At first, in the dream I heard a soft sound, something like wind blowing but someone talking in the distance. The voices were barely discernible from the constant winds. Then my father and mother appeared; slowly at first, as though coming out of a fog, a real thick fog. They didn't seem to walk; they just floated toward me in azureblue garments. I say garments because I associate the word 'garments' with biblical connotations. The garments were more of a type of robe than anything else.

"My father came to a position near the bunk I was sleeping on; at least I hope I was asleep; and yet I can remember seeing the sink just beneath my mother's robe edge, like she was a small figure hovering, above the sink, in a mist. My father took a hold of my hand and said, 'Come. Dottie wants you to be with us.' I remember that distinctly because he repeated it about four or five times. Then mom started saying, 'No, Calvin, he's got to finish this.' Then my father started walking away, or actually, floating away and I begged them to take me with them. 'Take me with you mother!' I kept crying and finally I awoke saying this very thing. When I awoke my throat was tight and my eyes and face were swollen and covered with my tears.

"I was still mentally sad when I awoke and couldn't help it so I cried for about five or ten minutes. I didn't tell about it because I felt ashamed. I don't know why but I felt ashamed."

The Cat was a descriptive nickname given to White Hawk by several students at the Shattuck School in Faribault, Minnesota, when he studied there. Following his graduation from the private boarding school, White Hawk entered the University of South Dakota at Vermillion as a freshman with aspirations of becoming a medical doctor. On Monday, March 25, 1968, three months after his sentence to death, he wrote about the following dream:

"This morning I had a dream which again involved cats. These cats were two medium-sized mountain lions; around a hundred and thirty or forty pounds. There were also many squirrels in the dream.

"I was sitting in a grain bin somewhere along a creek. Now that I retrospect I think the creek resembled that type of creek which was to the west of my uncle's milking barn.

"The trees, large cottonwoods which were shedding seeds, were the homes of many squirrels. I was hunting these squirrels but didn't get any, or kill any that is.

"As I was looking out from my hiding place I saw what looked like extra large squirrels; actually they were tails of the two lions but the bodies of the lions were well camouflaged from my view. I shot at the 'tails' and didn't hit them. The noise caused the squirrels to skirmish to their homes. When the lions showed themselves to me in the dream, I exploded — that is I went into a temper tantrum and yelled and yelled at the lions for spoiling my 'hunt.' Finally I commenced to shoot at them many times but couldn't strike anything. Although they just stood there and watched me, I could not strike them.

"Finally I jumped in the creek to cool off, but remained angered. I just stood in the water and looked up at the cats; they were perched gazing at me."

Joseph Satten, a psychiatrist from the Menninger Clinic, reported that White Hawk had dreams which involved "his dead parents before him and his asking them to take him with them, but they leave without him, while his mother looks back sadly, and he awakens crying . . . many of his early fantasies and memories suggest that sex and violent behavior are linked together in his mind."

Sunday morning in the guest room.

In his sleep Beaulieu heard the door click open. He rolled over on his back, opened his eyes, and focused on the bleached face of Reverend Beacher Givens, who was leaning over the bed dressed in his black robe and swinging a large stainless steel cross on an oversized chain, inches from his nose.

"Church time?" asked Beaulieu, ducking the cross.

"Mother flood time," said Beacher.

"Mother Beacher," moaned Beaulieu as he caught the swinging cross in one hand and sat up in bed. "Beacher, what is it we should talk about now? Do your followers know how peculiar you are in your vestments?"

"What choice is there here for them?"

"Part prairie parish banishment," said Beaulieu.

"Did we ever tell you . . ."

"Now wait a minute, who is this *we*?"

"Mother on the morning of the flood," said Beacher, reseating the thick spectacles on his short nose. "This morning mother and me. . . . Now, did *we* tell you, writers think they are so smooth, what we have never told anyone before?"

"What? *We* asked," he asked.

"On Good Friday White Hawk called me from the Yeado house

and asked me when were services. . . . He sounded troubled so
we asked him if he needed a dialogue, and after a short pause he
said *no* and hung up."

"So, is that it?"

"There is more," said the minister, fingering his cross and chain.
He sat on the bed. The muscles in his face were motionless as he
spoke. "He gathered blood from the dead man and baked it, in a
pan, in the oven. Demonic ritual. God it was Good Friday. Was it
his crucifixion commemoration? He must have been possessed with
evil. . . . There is no more to tell now."

Beaulieu rolled over in bed but he could not return to sleep. He
was thinking about the strange people who once surrounded and
influenced the tribal murderer. The orphan was loved and hated,
mistrusted and feared, used and abused to fulfill the aspirations and
needs of others, and seen as a saint and a sinner, malevolent, and
touched with evil.

Satten reported in a case summary that White Hawk "recalls trying to clean the blood off the floor, and then for some reason he
cannot understand, putting the blood-filled pans back where he
found them." White Hawk then wrapped James Yeado in a carpet,
and for unknown reasons, "took a pillow and put it under his head."

Reverend Givens was delivering his sermon. His dramatic voice
bounded over his few contributors at the dawn service, over the
unnatural pond, through the chapel stones, across the vacant lot
and through the trees into the window of the guest room. Beacher
was telling about a meeting he had the day before with two "street
saints working to save the life of a condemned man. . . . Clement
Beaulieu, a distinguished writer, and Douglas Hall, a truly great
humanitarian lawyer.

"Yesterday, I was with these fine and dedicated people, who,
without personal reward, were the stewards of good conscience . . .
we must act the same, acting as stewards. . . .

"Education is one good place to begin. You know my stand on
capital punishment and I will feel great guilt if I have not done
everything I can to fight capital punishment. . . ."

Beaulieu focused on the trees outside the window and listened to the ministerial aggrandizements. He questioned if religion and culture were possible without invoking the patrol saints of guilt and shame.

Daisie entered the room and sat on the bed.

"Well," he exclaimed, "this has become an unusual morning in the guest room. In comes the preacher with his massive cross and then his red-haired wife." Beaulieu was nervous. He turned from the window and scratched his head. Daisie was dressed in an oversized sweat shirt, but not oversized enough to hide the enormous size of her breasts. She was breathing hard from climbing the stairs.

"Now," said Beaulieu, "what I have in mind is conversation, good conversation. Personal and intimate to be sure, but nothing more than conversation. Under different circumstances, perhaps more, but for now let me get dressed and downstairs before mister morals returns from the pond. . . ."

"The pond?" she questioned.

"I mean the church. . . . Does he fish?"

"He talks and he talks too much."

"We should talk about your love for White Hawk while Beacher is gone," Beaulieu suggested. "Your love must be important to him."

Daisie was so eager to tell about her experiences that she began talking about herself, her marriage, her loves, and others, without questions, directions, or agreements. She needed more a listener than a lover.

"October," she said, starting with a fresh smile. "In October, White Hawk took my hand through the bars and said he was falling in love with me. I told him it was only mental but day after day, when I brought him food and things, I could feel my love growing for him. He was so powerful, so much a man. . . . It was something we could see in our eyes. Our love gave him something to live for, it gave him hope. . . ."

Her love, Beaulieu thought to himself, gave White Hawk another cultural and emotional burden. He met her needs for love at the expense of his own desperate needs. He met her needs from a prison cell, while waiting for the death sentence.

Daisie showed the writer two love letters from White Hawk. He had written them to her a few weeks before he was sentenced to death. He wrote to her as "Honey . . . take care of yourself physically and mentally." He wrote that love gave him reasons to live. He expressed his anxieties that her love would not last for him when he was sentenced. White Hawk wrote that he would take the time to be cured, "it will take one, two, or three years." The letters were passed through the bars when she visited. She burned all but two letters.

"Does your husband know about your love?"

"Yes, he found an unfinished letter I was writing to Tom and then he knew. . . . Well, I told him the truth about our love and he said that Tom was not capable of any feeling and then he said we were both sick. . . .

"From then on we visited Tom together and when we were there Tom would not show me his love, so Beacher would say, 'See, he has no feelings for you,' but when I would catch Tom's eye, the secret way, we knew our love was still alive.

"Beacher is a good person," she continued while she ran her hands through her hair. "He is a very objective person and a good provider, but he is not warm. He has never given me the kind of feeling I have had with Tom. . . . Tom has five children you know. . . ."

"But White Hawk is a prisoner," said Beaulieu.

"We have decided to give our marriage a two-year trial and if nothing changes, well, then we'll part and I'll wait for Tom. . . . I love him and doubt if anything will change."

Beacher heard his wife talking. He moved in silence through the kitchen closer to the drawing room where he could listen without being seen. When she spoke about him his blood pressure increased, and he could hear and feel his heart pounding in his head.

When the sermons ended Beaulieu packed his suitcase to leave the prairie and return to Minnesota.

"Come back soon, the door is always open to you," said Daisie. Beacher doubled her invitation as he walked the writer to his car. He touched the writer and then asked him in a hushed voice to drive around the corner behind the chapel, "where the two of us can have a private talk."

Beaulieu drove around the corner and heard the other side of loneliness. "She is a child, emotionally immature," he said as he removed his spectacles. His eyes seemed to shrink in size. "But otherwise she is a very mature woman. . . . She married the myth of the minister and was disappointed when she heard me swear for the first time. . . .

"But I am a subtle person about our problems. . . . Well, except when I found out about what she and White Hawk were doing. . . . She left a half-finished letter out on the table, and, well, she must have wanted me to find it and read it, how could I not see it there? The letter was to White Hawk.

"The next morning I went down to the jail and warned White Hawk, I shook my finger at him to keep his hands off my wife or I would not help him save his life. . . .

"Tell me, how stupid was that? Here was White Hawk behind bars, facing the death sentence, and I blame him for chasing after my wife behind my back. How can I blame him for Daisie being a willing child. . . . I came back later and apologized to him for what I had said in a rage. He said he could understand my feelings. . . .

"But both of them are sick. She goes for a condemned man behind bars, where she can control him and her feelings for him," said Beacher with tears in his eyes. "White Hawk, well, what is there left for him to call love?"

"But there must be something beautiful in their sickness," said Beaulieu. "Love is locked up all over this cruel prairie. . . ."

WORD WAR IN THE PARTSROOM

Morning winds pulled across the stiff grasses on the vernal prairie down from the sacred past into town. The wind smelled of horses. Appaloosa ponies wheeled out from dreams. The tribes danced with the winds through thunder clouds and retold in their oral traditions what was seen and heard.

James Yeado was known in his religious circle and main-street social coterie as a man who contained his fears and dreams. His closest friends, the pallbearers at his funeral, told more about their racial hatred for the tribal murderer than shared good memories about their dead friend.

Bertram Fredericks retired from his backyard automobile repair business; now he builds bird houses for his friends. He lives with his secretive wife in a small white house, scented with lilac and liniment, across the street from the courthouse.

When Clement Beaulieu arrived unannounced, the old man was in the garage cleaning his tools again, from the past three decades of use, and measuring the slow time to his second cigarette before noon. He was thin, bones showing, diabetic, and he labored over his breath.

143

"I am Clement Beaulieu," he said, standing on the doorframe waiting for an invitation to enter. The dark garage smelled sweet from petroleum which had penetrated the wooden workbenches and concrete floor.

The old man waited in silence.

"Clement Beaulieu from Minnesota," he said again, moving into the garage uninvited. Following a short pause, he turned his head down and to the side. "I am a writer and the murder of James Yeado was a terrible crime. He was a good man, an honest man, would you talk about your personal memories of him?"

Fredericks stared out the small window behind his workbench. He wiped his hands, a mindless ritual from his past as an automobile mechanic.

Beaulieu moved closer to the old man, turned and settled in the most comfortable of two chairs in the garage. A new unopened package of unfiltered cigarettes was on the table next to the chair.

Fredericks looked over from the window at the obtrusive writer sitting in his chair. He frowned, dropped the rag he had used to wipe his hands, looked toward the door and then moaned.

"Forgive me," said Beaulieu, at a captious moment of silence, and then moved from the personal chair to the straight-back wooden chair to show he was sensitive to the feelings of the old man.

"There are occasions when I smoke three before noon," said Fredericks when he lighted, with ceremonial care, his second cigarette that morning. His expression turned inward from the first inhalation. The smoke never seemed to leave his mouth or nose when he breathed.

"His best friends were his pallbearers and we carried him out to rest," he said, remembering the cold wind when he carried the coffin from the church.

"He was a good man. Kidded him a lot, you couldn't find anyone who didn't like him. . . . He didn't have an enemy in the world. He was a good church man and even way back in hard times he worked for the church. . . .

"We were his closest friends. At least once a week we played cribbage together and on Sundays, after church, we many times drove down to Sioux City, had dinner, and went to a movie. . . ."

He watched his cigarette burn between inhalations.

"Maybe a week before he died, me and the wife was over and he heard a noise outside, so he went out and when he came in he was white. . . . Those injuns were looking over his place, those injuns, the same ones, were in his garage then."

The ashes dropped in his lap.

"Those damned cops, they knew he wasn't in the church or in his store and his night light was on all day. . . . They should have gone over there before he was dead. . . . No one called the police."

The muscles in his thin cheeks twitched.

"When I think about it, she was up there, in the . . . Tied up all day, and those injuns didn't even have the decency to bring her any water."

His pale eyes filled with tears.

"She knew them injuns. . . . White Hawk bought a new ring in their store and he still owes them for it. . . . They got to do something about these things, but you can bet on yesterday being gone that those injuns won't die. . . ."

The old man shifted in his chair. The cigarette and his memories caused him to be anxious. He seemed more aggressive. He crushed the cigarette out, stood up and motioned to the writer to follow him through the door. Outside he walked toward the house past a pile of split wood.

"Chinese Elm, that stuff is tough," he said.

On the enclosed front porch the old man pointed toward the courthouse. He raised his arms, closed one eye, and aimed, as if he were holding a rifle, at the windows in the cellblock in the basement of the courthouse across the street. The silhouette of a prisoner moved in front of the glass.

"For hours we sat here on the porch watching those injuns, the women with them, the minister and his wife."

The old man paused, caught his breath three or four times and then, when he saw several young women walking near the courthouse, he said, expressing disdain in the tone of his voice, "the injuns used to yell out the window at the girls. Sometimes those teenage girls would go right up to the windows and talk to those killers."

He turned and stared at the writer.

"That damned Ramon Roubideaux will get those injuns off too, he gets them all off for killing," he said. Roubideaux is a successful tribal lawyer in South Dakota. He defended William Stands, who was in the Yeado home with White Hawk, winning an acquittal after two trials.

"We really miss them," he said as he opened the porch door and motioned the writer that it was time to leave. Outside, walking back past the wood pile, he said: "We had so much fun together. . . . It's been a long winter without them." He returned to the garage and closed the door without speaking.

Clifford Hinchman lived on a rural road south of town. The house was in need of paint and repairs. The lawn was covered with dead weeds and dandelions.

Beaulieu knocked on the front door. The screen was torn and tails of plastic used to cover the door during the winter were flapping in the wind. He heard footsteps start and stop, start and stop, and then the door opened.

Hinchman peered around the door.

"Beaulieu is my name, would you be so kind as to tell me a little about that terrible murder. . . . The good man who died was a jeweler, was he not?"

Hinchman locked the screen door. He looked up and down at the writer. Nothing on his face smiled. Fear pulled at the muscles on his thin neck. The tails of plastic flapped.

"Yeado, James Yeado, he was a home body sort, kept to himself most of the time," he said from behind the rusting screen. He held the door in both hands while he spoke in a strained voice.

"He would say he saw so many people all day he didn't want to see any more after work. . . . He closed the store, bought his meat downtown, and went home, what else is there to say? Nothing," he said and pulled back from the door.

He closed the door and then opened it again, saying: "Could you wait right there for a minute until I come back, in a minute?" He closed the door a second time. Beaulieu was suspicious and waited in his car a few minutes with the engine running before driving back into town to call on the third and last pallbearer on his list, pallbearers who were not related to the deceased.

Someone had called ahead to warn the pallbearers that a writer was asking questions about the murder.

Marshall Morrison worked for a car dealer. When Beaulieu entered the showroom late in the afternoon he was directed, as if his arrival had been expected, to the rear of the building where he found him waiting in a dark partsroom. The small room smelled from underarm perspiration and stale cigarette smoke.

Morrison slammed the door shut.

"How about this murder now," said Beaulieu.

"You communist fucker asking questions all around town to save that fuckin' injun killer," he said out of breath. He ground his teeth together between phrases. His green eyes, appearing small on his porcine face, focused like torch flames behind his unclean spectacles.

"You come from that communist civil liberties union, we can pound you and them bastards back east. . . . Where are you from commie lover, let me see some identification cards."

Beaulieu was an elected member of the Minnesota American Civil Liberties Union at the time. In the prairie red-neck manual of dangerous words and phrases, persons identified with the words *civil* and *liberties* or *eastern liberal*, which was anywhere east of Sioux Falls and the Minnesota border, were listed as communists and subversives. Beaulieu had become a factor in the prairie word war on communism.

Morrison shifted his weight from side to side, and rubbed his fat hands together. His skin squeaked from perspiration. "We ain't speaking about Yeado here, my wife worked for Yeado, and we ain't talking about him to no communist bastards."

"Your misfortune, because White Hawk speaks well of you all. . . . Shall we talk about him now?"

Morrison raised his trembling fat hands into round uneven fists. He opened his mouth and spread his lips to breathe. The coarse hairs on the back of his balding head were combed forward. His stomach, swelling from poor food and anxieties, dropped over his belt, and tore the last buckle hole.

Beaulieu was no match at that moment for the pallbearer, so he chose the role of the tribal trickster, the word warrior on the sacred road to outwit evil, in this case, evil in the partsroom. Beaulieu smiled and hummed ho ho ha ha ha ha haaaa. Morrison was breathing hard; he blocked the door with his swinish flesh.

When Morrison moved toward the writer, he reached with his right hand as the trickster into the inside pocket of his suit coat, as if he were reaching for a gun, still smiling and ho ho ha ha haaaaing, and told the partsman to hold his ground or be dead.

"I am an investigator for a secret government organization with the right to kill at will," said Beaulieu, with his hand still in his pocket. "You would not be the first on our list of too-bad-deads. . . . Now move aside, put your hands down and move away from that door. Should you speak to anyone about this, anyone, then you can count on me coming back one night to even the score. Now, sir, move aside."

Beaulieu shrugged his shoulders, smiled and hummed in the best tradition of tribal trickeries, and opened the door. "Remember what we said," he said, and pulled the partsroom door closed behind him.

Passing through the showroom on the way out of the building he paused to admire the automobiles. Smiling and humming at the main door, Beaulieu tipped his head, and then before leaving, raised his middle finger in an obscene gesture toward the salesmen on the floor.

PROSECUTORS

AND PRAIRIE FUN DANCERS

Prosecutor Charles Wolsky, Clay County Attorney, moved through conservative time and courtrooms as he once did over basketball courts. Discreet on the constitutional free-throws, passing few legal favors, calling fouls under the bench, and double dribbling down past the prairie juries.

In Armour, South Dakota, where William Stands was on trial for murder, Wolsky wagged his elbows as he once did with opponents beneath the basket and used his whole hand to emphasize legal points. He asked a prospective juror if he would be "kind of an umpire and call them the way you see them?" But the prosecutor was ponderous with his verbal shots and missed the hoop and lost the game at that trial.

Stands, who was defended by the celebrated tribal attorney Ramon Roubideaux, was acquitted after the jurors deliberated for more than ten hours. It was the second time the prosecutor lost the game. Stands was first tried for murder in Yankton, South Dakota, but the trial there ended without a score because the jurors could not agree on a verdict. Roubideaux, who was born on the reserva-

tion and decided to attend law school when a white bar owner refused to serve him because of his skin color, argues with the balance
and good humor of a shrewd trickster, and has won more murder
trials than most other lawyers on the prairie.

Wolsky grew up on a farm in North Dakota and earned his law
degree from the University of South Dakota. Soon after he passed
the state bar examination he ran for county attorney as an independent candidate and won. He believes that capital punishment is a
deterrence to crime. The prosecutor has a wide smile, but he seldom
seems at ease when he is speaking or listening to others. His full
round face and thick lips, not much chin, seem to shiver when he
argues in court. He shivers when witnesses are evasive.

In Armour while the jurors were deliberating, the prosecutor was
standoffish when he was invited with good humor to take a hand in a
poker game in the courthouse. Sheriff Nelson, his deputy Leonard
Andera, Roubideaux, who told irreverent but affectionate stories
about the white world of criminal justice, Clement Beaulieu, and
two other officers of the court, played poker while the jury deliberated. Wolsky was critical of the pastime and the place of the game.
He did not then know that the poker chips used in the game were
made from paper torn out of old legal books. Roubideaux won the
poker game and an acquittal for William Stands. Wolsky was not a
good loser; dark circles folded under his eyes when the jurors stated
the verdict.

Meanwhile, White Hawk, who had confessed to premeditated
murder, and then later changed his plea, was waiting on death row
for a trial. Minneapolis Attorney Douglas Hall represented his legal
appeals. The first was a commutation hearing before the South Dakota Board of Pardons and Paroles which was held at the penitentiary in Sioux Falls. The purpose of the hearing was not to argue the
state capital punishment statute but to determine whether the sentence was more severe than was proper under the law and whether
the sentence should be commuted to life imprisonment. White
Hawk was sentenced to death on a guilty plea without a trial.

Douglas Hall, the determined liberal gentleman, the juridical humanist, counselor for good and bad dreams, set aside his favorite pipe and called the first witness at the commutation hearing.

Frank Duchenau, from Eagle Butte, South Dakota, leaned back in the witness chair. News reporters were seated behind the witness. In front of the witness, against the wall near the prosecutor sat Charles White Hawk, uncle to Thomas, with his arms folded over his massive chest. Old White Hawk owned a small cattle ranch on the reservation. He seldom spoke. During the hearing he sat facing all the witnesses and watched the expressions with their words.

"I am chairman of the Cheyenne River Sioux Tribe," said Ducheneau, gesturing with his lips toward the old man against the wall who was watching him, "and also the President of the United Sioux Tribes of South Dakota representing some thirty-five thousand Sioux Indians. . . .

"I am here today to beg of this honorable body that they consider the appeal of many people of this country for the commutation of the death sentence of Thomas James White Hawk. We also want you to know that we do not condone what he has done. . . .

"I have never believed in capital punishment, whether it be White Hawk or anybody else. God has given us life and he should be the one to take it away. Each and every one of us sometime in our life has done something wrong and are sorry we did it and would give anything to undo it. . . .

"It has not been too long ago that our men were killed and our women were raped while their husbands looked on helplessly because they were held prisoner. The only way the women had to protect themselves was to fill their bodies with sand. These stories were told to us by our fathers and mothers. Our people did not believe in capital punishment. If murder was committed by someone he was compelled to make amends to the family or to be banished from the tribe for life. . . ."

Ducheneau was the first of twenty-seven witnesses who opposed capital punishment and the death sentence for White Hawk. Episcopal Bishop Lyman Ogilby and Reverend Russell Tarver testified from their hearts and from their positions as church leaders, but most of the witnesses who testified at the hearing were tribal people from various organizations and reservations.

Bishop Ogilby read a resolution emphasizing that the taking of human life was not within the right of man, "therefore, be it resolved that the General Convention of the Episcopal Church goes on record as opposed to capital punishment . . . the South Dakota Council urges the Board of Pardons and Paroles and the Governor of South Dakota to commute the death sentence of Thomas White Hawk."

Reverend Tarver, pastor of the First United Methodist Church in Vermillion, represented the Bishop of the United Methodist Church of North and South Dakota. Reading from a prepared statement he was the most organized witness to appear at the hearing. "One, no one has been executed by the State of South Dakota. Two, a careful analysis of the news media would indicate that contrary to popular opinion there have been other crimes of comparable senseless brutality over the past twenty years in South Dakota not punished by death. Three, a careful analysis of the court records would indicate that there has been inequity in the courts of South Dakota with the Indian Americans. . . . It is the function of the penal system to punish the offender, protect society and where possible rehabilitate the criminal. . . . Nothing can bring a gentle and kind James Yeado back to life. Two wrongs do not make a right. . . . My plea is for the life of a man, not for his freedom."

Charles Wolsky was not in good humor. He mentioned, while waiting for the hearing to begin, the low salaries for elected court officials and complained that the demands of the Stands and White Hawk cases took so much of his time that he could not attend to other legal business. He had not been successful in finding a tribal person to speak for the prosecution. But at the last minute he announced that he would call a surprise tribal witness who would support capital punishment.

Close to a hundred tribal people gathered for the hearing, most to support the witnesses, but the warden would not permit more than a few people in the waiting room of the penitentiary at a time.

Prison guards and local law enforcement officials were nervous about so many tribal people at the hearing.

Snow was falling, the wind was cutting cold, it was the middle of the winter and the tribal people crowded together and waited outside in parked cars. The people dreamed and told stories in celebration of their new tribal union.

Ronald Libertus, representing various urban tribal organizations, testified that because of the racial inequities in the legal system "we should never under any circumstances execute a minority person, and because of the cruel and inhuman treatment that is inflicted by capital punishment itself, this action should never be carried out."

Twilo Martin, University of North Dakota Indian Association, protested the death sentence. Her voice was emotional. "We are not voicing this protest only because Thomas White Hawk is an Indian, even though it was a white man who tried to teach the Indian it is wrong to take the life for a life yet how little he values his own code, but because we feel every human being has a right to live. . . .

"I tried to differentiate between my emotional self and realistic self when I was walking up here, and I suppose no matter what I say, you know, it's not going to matter any because I tried to be emotional. . . .

"Maybe it is because I lived on the reservation all my life. I know what it is like to be there and what the kids are going through in school right now, Indian students there and without somebody trying to understand them and saying we are being emotional about it. . . . So everybody can go on facts, but I think emotion counts also in this case and the cases of all other Indian students, I know. . . ."

Melvin Tom, Walker River Paiute, representing the Coalition of American Indian Citizens, reported that he was concerned that "another injustice is being done to one of our fellow Indians. It is an injustice that has come about because of the relationship between Indians and whites . . . whites being the dominant and controlling people in this country. . . . It is most of the time easier to submit to the system than it is to fight it. . . ."

Sister Agnes Center, Mount Marty College in Yankton, South
Dakota, told the Board of Pardons and Paroles that she was a "fullblood Sioux Indian . . . from the Pine Ridge Reservation. I mainly
want to recommend or ask for commutation for the death sentence
of Thomas White Hawk on the grounds of human interest, and also
I would like to put a plea in for a greater understanding for cultural
differences among our racial groups and also in the interest of re-
habilitation for Indians for greater understanding and also of mental
illness in our socieities."

Clement Beaulieu, then a staff writer for the *Minneapolis Tribune*,
testified in confusing verbal circles about tribal identities and unconscious lives. Douglas Hall asked him to restate one answer and
then let him plow over his own deluge of emotional words. He was
nervous, spoke too soon new thoughts, and seemed to fall through
his best metaphors, somewhere between emotions and abstractions.
The prosecutor, who had been critical of his writing about White
Hawk and the case, frowned while he testified and then dropped
his head from time to time as if he were biting his tongue or swal-
lowing his rage.

"Tom was involved in a conflict of his own identity, his own
unconscious life of Indian identity and his pursuit and involvement
in the demands and expectations of the dominant white society,"
said Beaulieu shifting forward in his chair. "I saw it in myself. I
saw it in many other Indian people and felt that it was a precedent
that I wanted to address my energy to in terms of writing, that is,
I wanted to make a statement that a great many Indian people in
this country suffer from this same conflict, in the sense of cultural
schizophrenia. . . . The very society which creates the sickness in
which Indians have had to live . . . is the very society which now
every day becomes the doctor . . . a man cannot be condemned
by an institution of that dominant culture which has actually led
to the problems he has to live with. . . ."

The prosecutor was irritated and pinched his large lips closed as
if each word from the witness caused a sour taste in his mouth. Then
he stood his ground near the hearing table, hiking up his trousers,

smacked his yellow legal pad with his open hand, and started his foul-shot examination. He challenged the writer witness on his facts about White Hawk, statements about racism in South Dakota, and referred to several published newspaper stories the witness had written about Dane White, a tribal child who hanged himself in a jail cell where he had been held for more than a month as a truant.

Wolsky: Who told you that all Indians are like warts and the only way you can get rid of them is burn them off? [Referring to a pamphlet written by Beaulieu.]

Beaulieu: A man in Vermillion.

Wolsky: What was his name?

Beaulieu: Because I did not use his name in the pamphlet, I will not use his name here.

Wolsky: You call that pamphlet an accurate presentation of the facts, is that correct?

Beaulieu: Yes. I said a man in Vermillion. . . .

Wolsky: You didn't say anything. . . .

Hall: Just a minute, Mister Wolsky. You are not asking questions now, you are badgering the witness.

Wolsky: What did you have to do with this [reference to the Dane White suicide], I understand you have done some investigation as far as a young man hanging himself in jail of recently, is that correct?

Beaulieu: Yes.

Wolsky: In other words, you are a cause hunter. . . .

Silence.

Tillie Walker, United Scholarship Service, testified that White Hawk was receiving educational assistance while he was a student at Shattuck School in Faribault, Minnesota. "I feel that Thomas White Hawk is part of the family. . . ."

Wolsky: So because of this personal feeling you would perhaps overlook some of the things that the law is really concerned with in this case?

Walker: I am thinking about a human being who is condemned to die.

Wolsky: This is why you are for commutation because you don't think he should die, you are against capital punishment isn't that correct?

Walker: That is right.

Wolsky: It wouldn't really matter what the facts or circumstances . . . you would still be for commutation because you are just against capital punishment?

Walker: I think that in this case he has not had a chance really for a fair trial. I don't think Thomas White Hawk has had justice in the state of South Dakota. . . .

Wolsky: Have you talked to the judge?

Walker: I don't know the judge, sir. . . .

Wolsky: You have read the newspapers?

Walker: Yes, I have.

Wolsky: Is that what you base your opinion on?

Walker: I base my opinion on the fact that you do not know Thomas White Hawk. You do not know what he came up through. You do not know the community where he grew up. . . .

Wolsky: Well, have you been there all the time when he is experiencing all these things?

Walker: I grew up on an Indian reservation.

Wolsky: Does that make all Indians the same?

Walker: No, it does not make us all the same, but I think we have a lot of feeling for Thomas White Hawk. . . .

Thomas White Hawk had fallen from tribal grace for his terrible crimes but he would not be forgotten or banished. The witnesses brought him back to the families. Now he must show concern for the harm he has caused the world.

Douglas Hall, the eternal optimist, leaned back in his chair, crossed his long legs, lighted his pipe, and smiled at Charles White Hawk who was still sitting across the hearing room with his arms folded over his massive chest. Hall felt good about the passions and energies that had been expressed by the witnesses. It was an honest and emotional hearing, he said. No one was aware then that he was losing his sanctioned place as a senior partner in a prestigious law firm, the firm he had organized during his work in union law, because he had been representing too many people who could not afford the high cost of legal services. Several months later he was asked to leave the firm.

Outside in the penitentiary parking lot the windows in some of the cars were frosted on the inside. Tribal witnesses and supporters were waiting in the cold and telling stories and wondering who would be the secret witness for the prosecution.

"George Wallace."

"The Commissioner of Indian Affairs."

"Some prairie fun dancer."

"Damn my feet are cold," said Clement Beaulieu. He tapped his feet together and began telling about a racist motel manager and a dream he had the night before the hearing. "This is like a reservation in a parking lot. . . . Because I am a mixedblood this motel manager in Vermillion took me for white, and while I was filling out the registration card he commented on my occupation. I had put down that I was a newspaper writer, which I am, and he asked me what I was writing about and I told him White Hawk and that was enough to get him going. He said, 'All these injuns around here, they're just a gimmie people, gimmie, gimmie all the time, waiting for the dole. . . . You take them on the reservation, give them two bucks and they're drunk for sure. What a waste of land, gotta be a more profitable way to use the land than for the injuns,' and then he said the good one, the one the fat-lipped prosecutor wanted to know about, 'The injuns in South Dakota are like warts, if you can't burn them off, then you gotta make them beauty marks.'

"When he finished out of breath, with his eyes big, I asked him if he had ever heard about the coming of the new tribal shamans and the ghost dance. He said, 'Nope, never heard about that,' so, after a short pause, I told him that the ghost dancers had the dreams for the best use of the land. 'What's that?' he asked. 'All but cedar trees, the few that remain standing, and the tribes, will be buried beneath a new earth. White people gone forever and the buffalo will come back.' The telephone rang, he turned to answer it, and I left for my room."

Beaulieu rubbed his hands together.

"But this dream two nights ago scared the shit out of me. Start the engine again, the heater is cold. Prisons are the coldest places in the underworld. Well, I was on this ship or pleasure cruiser when several white people with short hair rushed up to me and cursed and threatened me because White Hawk had escaped from death row. Two close friends of the Yeados', two pallbearers, forced me to take a gun, a rifle, because White Hawk was armed. The white people screamed at me, 'This is all your fault because you wrote about him and he is still alive now to kill other people, this is all your fault!' They tried to shame me into being responsible for their racial fear and hatred. They wanted me to shoot and kill White Hawk because I wrote about him and saved him from the electric chair, before he killed more white people.

"Except for the bow, the cruiser was enclosed with windows. I was standing on the inside when I saw White Hawk creeping on the outside deck past the windows. I watched him. White people were screaming at me. White Hawk was holding a rifle, the same one he used in the murder. When he raised his weapon and started to run outside the windows toward the bow of the cruiser, I raised the rifle the two pallbearers had given me and followed White Hawk in the sight. White people were screaming, 'Shoot him, shoot him, before he kills again, you set him free, now you kill him!'"

"I followed him in the sight, 'Kill him you goddam liberal commie, kill him,' but I could not squeeze the trigger. I was aiming at his head but I could not fire the rifle, and then White Hawk disappeared where the windows ended."

Silence.

Libertus told about driving down to Vermillion with Beaulieu the first time, a few days after White Hawk had been sentenced to death. "It was in the winter and cold, like this, last year in fact, and the heater was out on the car. Not knowing what to expect, we were both quiet when we crossed the border. Then it happened. South of Sioux Falls, on a four-lane highway, a giant bird, a hawk, raised up from the center of the road, wings spread wide open. I hit the brakes but the hawk was killed when he hit the grill. . . . Terrible omen we thought then. When we stopped to examine the accident we saw where the huge hawk wings had spread from fender to fender across the front of the car. The wings of the hawk left marks in the road dirt and salt on the car. Wing feather marks wrapped around the fenders. Here we are now."

On the second day of the commutation hearing the prosecutor called his secret and sole witness, the last witness to speak at the hearing before the Board of Pardons and Paroles.

Wolsky: State your name. . . .

McGaa: M. Edward McGaa. . . .

Wolsky: What is your present occupation?

McGaa: Law student at the University of South Dakota. Also assistant to the director of the Institute of Indian Studies, University of South Dakota.

Wolsky: What year are you in law school?

McGaa: Second year.

Wolsky: Would you tell us what percent you are Indian?

McGaa: I am half Indian. My parents are both half and half. . . .

Wolsky: Where were you raised?

McGaa: I was born at Pine Ridge and I was raised in Rapid City. My folks left the reservation and my dad is a common laborer. . . .

Wolsky: And you have been in the service?

McGaa: I graduated from Rapid City High School. I put in to the Bureau of Indian Affairs for a scholarship to go to college. My folks didn't have enough money to send me to school. I never heard from them, so I joined the Marines for two years. . . .

Wolsky: Well, after your enlisted days?

McGaa: Well, first I enlisted for two years. I got out and went to college and graduated from St. John's University. Then I went back in because I wanted to fly. I always wanted to fly planes, so I went through OCS [Officers Candidate School]. That was for three months. That was pretty tough. . . . They weeded out half of them there. Then I put in for flight training. They weeded out half of them there. That lasted a year and a half. I got my wings. Then

I became a helicopter pilot and I flew the helicopter two or three years roughly. . . . I always wanted to fly jets, so I put in for the jet program. . . . I flew one hundred and ten missions in Vietnam. Several medals. I was requested to stay in. I would have been a major but the reason I got out was that I would see the reservation. I always go to the sundance and I danced Indian. . . .

Wolsky: And have you formed an opinion as to the commutation of White Hawk's sentence?

McGaa: Yes, I have formed an opinion.

Wolsky: And based upon the facts of the case, the facts as you know them, what is your opinion?

McGaa: Well, I formed my opinion because of the old Indian way, the traditional Indian method from the facts of the case.

Wolsky: Would you explain that?

McGaa: Well, the old-time Indian had three main methods of punishment. We had outright capital punishment. We had banishment or we had forgiveness. The forgiveness portion was completely unlike white law. . . . But, banishment was usually when you did something to your people. They would banish you from the tribe.

"Well, this is actually a death sentence because you were cast alone on the cold, harsh prairie in those days, and you were just a prize for trophy-seeking enemies. You had nobody to defend you. The outright death penalty was when the tribe would kill you for a real grave serious crime where you brought tremendous disgrace and despair upon your people. . . ."

McGaa, who became more and more uncomfortable in the witness chair, was then examined by Gordon Hayes, member of the Board of Pardons and Paroles, from Pierre, South Dakota.

Hayes: Suppose you're satisfied that White Hawk had a mental illness and that mental illness contributed to what happened in the Yeado home, the murder and rape, so that he was a sick man at the time, would you favor the death sentence under those circumstances?

McGaa: I don't know that much about mental illness. . . .

Hayes: Well, just on those facts assuming you were convinced of those various factors, would you be in favor of the death penalty for an ill man?

McGaa: For a mentally ill man?

Hayes: Yes.

McGaa: I don't know. I really don't know. The old-time Indians, I don't know, they looked at the crime and they gave out the death sentence, and I have always tried to think like the old-time Indian. . . .

Hayes: Well, we are faced with a particular kind of punishment assuming a man to have a mental illness. The problem here is, should the punishment be execution?

McGaa: That's a tough question for me to answer.

Joseph Satten, from the Menninger Clinic, concluded in his report that White Hawk "has been suffering from a long-standing psychiatric condition, however labeled, with a tendency to lapse into transient dream-like or psychotic-like episodes and . . . had lapsed into such an episode during a significant part of the time that he was in the Yeado house. . . ."

Satten pointed out in the case summary of his examination that White Hawk had aspirations of becoming a doctor but was not sure he could accomplish that goal. White Hawk entered the Shattuck School in Minnesota and was an "outstanding athlete there, but he tended to keep to himself. . . . While on the athletic field, he was hit on the head with a shot put and required sutures to repair the laceration. Six months after that injury, when he returned to school the following fall, he began to have severe migraine headaches with disturbances in his vision, and he frequently reported to the physician . . . for medication to ease the pain and the tension. Also to ease the tension, he found himself playing football very hard, and occasionally he was knocked out on the field. . . ."

White Hawk was examined while he was waiting on death row. Satten reported that the "illness seems clearly to be related to three groups of forces operating on this young man. The first, consisting of his early familial and environmental experiences, were of the type and intensity that are frequently linked to the development of later mental illness in almost any individual. Secondly, his experience of the conflict of cultures that a member of any minority group experiences in relationship to the larger culture only tends to accentuate the personal factors leading to illness. Thirdly, and of lesser importance in the mind of this examiner, are the factors relating to his specific identity as an Indian. His Indian background would tend to make him place a high value on stoicism, emotional impassivity, withdrawal, aloofness, and the denial of dependence on others. In addition, the tendency of some in the dominant culture to devaluate Indians and the Indian culture would tend to accentuate his feelings of loneliness and suspicion. All of these forces, however, tend to operate in the same direction, toward precipitating and perpetuating mental difficulties. . . ."

When McGaa was dismissed as a prosecution witness he wasted no time leaving the hearing room. Outside, in the hall where several news reporters were waiting, he looked back toward the hearing room, motioned with nervous gestures, and asked Clement Beaulieu, "Who was that old man in there?"

"Charles White Hawk."

"White Hawk, White Hawk," exclaimed McGaa, gesturing with sudden hand movements, "That old man is a medicine man and he was doing his power on me in there. . . ."

"Power on the prairie fun dancers."

Governor Frank Farrar was overwhelmed with letters critical of capital punishment. The governor called a press conference, several months after the postconviction hearing, and announced in a firm and somber voice that he was commuting the death sentence imposed on White Hawk.

"I must say that during the many years I served as a practicing attorney, county judge, and attorney general of this state, no case has come before me which presented such a brutal crime and total disrespect for human life as the murder for which Thomas James White Hawk now serves in the state penitentiary.

"This case has inspired more public interest than any other question in the state of South Dakota for decades.

"The case, from time of commitment, has placed difficult burdens on public officials at all levels of government.

"Yet, none of us involved in the process of justice, has suffered more painfully than the widow and family of James Yeado, along with his many relatives and friends. For them, we must all offer our continuing prayers and comfort.

"This case has also been painful for the friends and relatives of Thomas James White Hawk who stepped in to help a lonely Indian boy try to adjust to the loss of both parents and escape from impoverished conditions which plagued him throughout life. . . .

"Even in the light of this tragic crime, perhaps one positive development has come from this entire case; focusing the attention of the nation on the plight of some of our Indian people who have lived for decades under federal control in poverty and in many cases less than human dignity.

"Thomas James White Hawk is a product of a tragic social environment. Unlike the majority of American youth, he was denied the full benefits of parental direction because of their death during his formative years.

"In addition, Thomas James White Hawk suffered some traumatic personal experiences along with a severe head injury during his youth.

"All of these factors could have conspired to motivate the brutal crime for which he now pays his debt to society. . . .

"While I favor the retention of the capital punishment laws on the books for whatever deterrent value and use in future cases they might have, the imposition of a life sentence can be punishment equally as severe to the defendant as the death penalty. Having to live and face daily the inhumane act may be for the defendant as great a punishment as death itself. . . .

"I have reviewed the case of Thomas James White Hawk giving it my careful and prayerful consideration. Just prior to this statement, I have advised officials of the South Dakota State Penitentiary to convey to Mr. Thomas James White Hawk that I have on this 24th day of October, 1969, commuted his sentence of death in the electric chair to a sentence of life imprisonment for so long as he shall live with the personal request to future Boards of Pardons and Paroles that all petitions for further commutation of the sentence of the named defendant be denied."

White Hawk was shaving when he was told that his sentence had been commuted. Later, he wrote the following in a letter to his friend Sister Agnes Center, who was then working at the Red Cloud Indian School on the Pine Ridge Reservation.

South Dakota State Penitentiary

October 27, 1969   Register Number 16251   Censor 6

Dear Agnes:

When I was told, I was about to shave, but I went completely numb. I shaved, washed up, and put my towel in my cell. Finally, the impact struck me and I completely broke down. I felt as though a tremendous load, almost a physically perceivable load, was lifted from my shoulders, making my body feel real light. . . . I'm still in the process of gathering my emotional wares back together. . . .

As you know by now, I'm now out in the population, that is, with the other inmates. It's very nice just to be around people again—I didn't realize just how much I missed them until I met many of them. . . .

The next week or two, I will just take things easy, get used to the place. It's very different from being locked up all day. Not that we're free to roam the cell blocks all day—we're not. But, for me at least, this new freedom I'm appreciative of. . . .

Affectionately Yours,

Tom